THE FOREVER ENEMY

Suzie Ivy

ISBN-13: 978-1-946256-34-8

Cover design by: Fantasia Frog Designs
Printed in the United States of America

To Molly
May you find all the bones in heaven.

FOREVER

Names have been changed to protect the guilty.

Good detectives fight each day to protect the innocent.

K9s protect their handlers.

Meet the dogs of forever.

Suii, Bell, Sugarplum, and introduing Rat Cat who wants to be a K9s irritating sidekick.

CHAPTER ONE

I hear Bell growling from the back patio again and I decide losing my mind is the perfect option. The past two weeks, after a pleasant vacation of doing pretty much nothing, have been hectic and in the case of Bell and the back patio, ridiculous.

I close my eyes and rub my temples while breathing deeply. When I open them again, the growling with an occasional high-pitched bark still annoys my eardrums. I walk to the back door and look out to see exactly what I expected.

Bell's new personal demon is at it again.

"Bell, no," I say after opening the door. My trusted K9 doesn't even look at me. She's turned toward the block wall that we share with our new neighbors. The object of her pain and the scourge of our condo community sits on top of our shared wall, licking his feline paws in all his king-like orange marmalade glory.

I call him Rat Cat to make Bell and me feel better. It works for me but Bell is still holding out on the name. I think she simply calls him Dinner.

Rat Cat came into our life along with the new neighbors from Virginia who bought Ed's condo. Maybe it's the fact the cat is Southern with a twang in its strangled meow that gets on my nerves so much. Not that Southern twangs get on my nerves because I actually like the sound, just not from a cat.

The feline in question has no idea the delightful snack he would make or that I would hide the evidence of his demise in a heartbeat. Dogs have grown on me and turned me into a K9 loving fool, but cats are just plain evil. Bell and I fully agree that we dislike any animal who thinks gloating from above makes them special.

"Come on, Bell; he won't leave until

you do." This is now our daily ritual.

Bell glances my way quickly before her attention snaps back to the cat. Neither budges from their game of thrones.

This has been going on for weeks, even during my vacation. The same ritual each morning and each night: Bell runs out the dog door to do her business. When Rat Cat first sees her, he raises his back and his hair stands on end. He throws out a hiss or two, waiting for Bell's counterthreat. At Bell's first growl, Rat Cat casually sits his prissy backside down on the wall and licks his paws. It's his way of letting Bell know her threats mean nothing.

And my K9 falls for it by continuing her promise of pending menace while Rat Cat cherishes every moment. It's pathetic.

"Bell, it's time to go to work," I finally say, using a command voice. Like previous mornings, this finally gets her attention. With a last solid bark, the teasing match disperses and she heads in my direction. Rat Cat casually turns his back, strolls down the length of the wall, and jumps into his own yard.

"Rat Cat twenty-two, Bell zero," I tell her.

Bell wags her tail like nothing unusual occurred. With a shake of my bewildered head, I strap her into her K9 vest. When the last piece of Velcro is firmly in place, I sit back and see a different dog. Her eyes tell me she's ready to work. She'll gladly give her life for mine if it's called for. This dog is ready to help fight crime and she knows exactly what that job entails.

"Rat Cat is beneath you," I say softly with a scratch under her chin. "His brains are smaller because his tiny little skull won't hold anything of real size. If you keep trying to coax him from the wall with growls and barks, you'll have the same outcome. My point is the same outcome each day makes you look bad and that's embarrassing. Rat Cat enjoys watching you salivate. You lose every time yet still go back for more. My philosophy is to ignore him and he'll go away." Wishful thinking on my part but maybe he'll run in front of a car, slowly.

Bad detective, I tell myself.

Bell, in turn, uses her personal K9 philosophy on me by ignoring my exceptional words of wisdom and running to my front door to get our workday started. I clip my gun and badge to my belt and follow Bell to our shiny white, non-marked detective vehicle.

It's a sunny pre-fall day with a slight lowering of temperature that signifies the coming change in seasons. I prefer summer, as a human should, and Bell prefers colder weather, as anyone with a permanent coat of fur should. On this, neither of us have a say and we take what's given.

While I absorb the sun and try to pretend it will be around for another few months, Bell jumps in the SUV after I open the back hatch and we're officially on duty. Detective Jolett, homicide division, and her faithful K9 companion, Bell. Unfortunately, my current assignment is not a homicide though maybe it could be if I lose my cool. I shouldn't smile at the thought. I really shouldn't.

This morning, I'm gathering town gossip to help solve my non-homicide case. I'm stuck on the case due to one of our property crimes detectives being on leave for his first baby. I'm not happy about the assignment but I get a paycheck each week and feel the need to earn it. It also doesn't help that this incident comes on the heels of my last large case involving high school students, my favorite age group, not! Hopefully, this next torture session will be over soon. Not that I hope we are overrun with homicides because that would be horrible but if the murders expected over the next few months could come at once, I could go back to full-time homicide and I'd be okay with it.

Right now, apprehending a window shooter is my main objective. For the investigation to come to fruition, I need someone to rat out a friend. It's a longshot but I'm fresh out of ideas. To get things rolling on my new plan, I'm going to stir up the gossip clutch and see if anyone breaks. I'll try to do this without blood or threats of disfigurement.

I chuckle softly while driving. In my opinion, my humor is wasted in today's world. I would have made such a great detective back in the mob days of the '40s and

'50s. At least I think so. "Someone messes with me, I'm gonna mess with them, right, Bell?" I say in my best Al Capone voice.

She lets out a bark in reply. Bell has seen the *Untouchables* as many times as me and knows all the one-liners too. She's just not a show-off.

The number one place in town for gossip is not where you might think. Women are not involved in spreading this gossip because women of any age don't hold a candle to old men. Watch the mob movie classics and you'll understand.

Where do you find old men at this time of the morning? That's easy. Lucky Gas and Wash, Lucky's for short, has the cheapest coffee in town which makes it the local gathering club for man gossip. Lucky Gas is also at the center of my case.

A week ago, the owner raised his coffee prices by a quarter. Even with the increase they still undercut everyone else in town by ten cents per hot, delicious cup and they include one free refill. Twenty-four hours after the announced increase, someone shot the front window of Lucky's with a .22 caliber bullet. The unique approach of the shooter was to aim dead center at the sign announcing the new price. This placement of the bullet is known as a clue and as any good detective would, I pay close attention to all aspects of crime. The unhappy customer shot the window while the store was closed and no one was inside. Of course, the culprit couldn't be positive no one was inside and they're lucky no one was hurt.

I pull into the gas station and find a spot to park. It's located on southwest corner of Main Street and Whippoorwill. The grayish storefront is not much to look at even with the newly replaced glass. It does, however, represent rural gas stations in most American small towns. It even has a fifty-foot pole with a U.S. flag waving in the slight breeze. With four pumps, it has double the number of the other place in town that sells gas. Lucky also has a drive-through car wash and it's made our lives easier at the department.

The police chief buys a yearly package from the owner and officers can run their vehicles through with zero out of pocket expense. Before the agreement, our cars were a sore point for the city council because they were not clean and shiny like the fire department's vehicles. I waited impatiently for someone to inform the misguided councilmen that if police officers had time to shine and polish their vehicles, we would need fewer police officers on the street, not more as our chief is requesting.

Of course, no one spoke up and like a good public servant, I kept my mouth closed and my chief happy.

I should mention we do have a box-cutter gas station run by some big wig corporation from out of state. It has twenty-four pumps and looks exactly like every other station the corporation owns. Locals call it the Tourist Trap, TT for short, because of the outrageously priced souvenirs ranging from petrified wood to T-shirts with ridiculous slogans like, "Buy a T-shirt, save a dinosaur." The station is kept alive by summer tourists and those driving through town on their way to who knows where. No self-respecting townie will be seen at TT.

"Good morning, Detective," one of the

men standing with the serial gossipers on the walkway says when he sees me. It interrupts my not enough coffee in the system brain and makes me focus on the problem at hand. He's given me the exact opening I needed.

"Good morning, gentlemen," I greet. The scraggly group has mostly unkempt hair if they have any, wrinkled clothing, and a pathetic need to avoid their spouses until a decent hour of the morning. Maybe until sometime after lunch if they're fortunate.

I meet their eyes one at a time before speaking. "I was hoping to talk to one of the clerks inside about what happened a few nights ago," I say cheerfully. The men lower their eyes, look around at the ground, and shuffle their feet, exactly as I expect. "Shooting a gun into a building even when it's closed is a felony and I plan to prosecute to the fullest," I tell them earnestly. No one calls me on the fact I don't prosecute cases and it's actually the job of the county attorney's office. These men aren't really thinking about my words; they're thinking about how to get away from me just as they do their wives.

Finally, one of them looks up. I believe his name is Leroy. He likes to call in complaints about music in cars being too loud and other problems that don't stick around long enough for an officer to track it down. Then he complains about the officer. There's a gap in his mouth where his eyetooth should be and his comb-over needs a few extra hairs to make it successful. "I heard it was a high school rival of our football team," he volunteers. "Seems like a juvenile thing to do if you ask me."

I smirk. The shooter was extremely juvenile and fits Leroy's character perfectly. He's high on my suspect list and just went up a notch by trying to pawn it off on kids. "That's a good observation," I say slowly and loudly so their selective hearing can pick it up. "If it wasn't for the fact the bullet hit dead center in the coffee price increase sign, and the threatening letter the following day, I might agree with you." I let my words sink in for a moment. "The only chance the culprit has for a lighter sentence is to come forward and explain themselves." The threatening letter was minimal and only said, "Your coffee doesn't taste good enough to be priced so high so change it or else." *Or else* is not a threat. *Or else* could mean I won't shop here. Added to the bullet hole though, it appears a tad bit darker. Maybe the two aren't connected but I'm guessing they are.

Jeb Garland, one of the smarmiest of the group, looks at me. I know Jeb because he's twice my age and enjoys flirting with women, unattached or married, regardless of age. He has about ten hairs on his head which he grows extra-long and doesn't bother combing over and just lets them stick up any old place they want to. His gut extends almost to his knees and he has a propensity to forget about bathing. Welcome to my single life. I would like to say he's harmless but he's made even me uncomfortable at times and several women in town have complained. "Probably a disgruntled customer," he grumbles and looks me up and down slowly with his lecherous eyes before glancing away.

I take a long breath without appearing to, I hope, and continue staring at Jeb until he looks my way again. "That's exactly what I think and I even have a lead." I give eye contact to each man again before saying, "Good day, gentlemen."

I walk back to my car, hoping they have enough coffee in their systems to allow their brains to function at a higher level so they realize I never went inside and spoke to the clerk.

At the exact time I grab the door handle, a loud whistle splits the air. It's known as a catcall and every woman on the planet grinds her teeth when it happens. I remove my hand from the door, then walk around to the back and open Bell's hatch. I clip on her lead and she jumps out. "It's time to work," I tell her softly.

With her at my side, I approach the men again. "I think you all know Bell."

Now they won't look at me and I allow my grin to widen. I unclip Bell's leash. "Hold," I command. She sits and focuses her attention on the group of men. "Gentlemen, I wouldn't move if I were you." I approach Jeb and step into his personal space. Of course, due to his belly, it's not as close as I would like but then his smell makes me reconsider and I step back a micro-inch. It doesn't help. "Would you like to whistle again?" I ask in my no-nonsense voice that should be used on children.

He looks down at his feet. "Most women take it as a sign of respect because all I'm saying is, you're hot."

I don't even need to think about my reply. "Hot is something that will burn you. Bell isn't in hold position to protect me. She's there so your friends can't leave without hearing my response and witnessing your lack of character. The reason I'm standing in front of you is because you think an obscene whistle is a sign of respect to a woman. Bell's a female and you are more her type than mine. Why don't you give her the same whistle and we'll see how that goes for you."

One of the men chuckles and Jeb throws him a dirty look. "You've made your point," he says testily.

That's what he thinks.

"No, actually, I haven't. If another woman complains about your ongoing dis-respect, I'll charge you with harassment. I doubt the charge will stick but it will cost you time and you'll possibly need an attorney which will cost you money. I, on the other hand, will be paid for every minute of my time in court. I hope I've made myself clear."

"Bell, release." I slap my side. She walks over and sits facing me while I attach her lead. This time I leave without saying goodbye.

I pull out of the gas station and head to the police department.

My cell rings as I drive into the lot. "Jolett, your friendly detective to the rescue," I answer because my screen says it's Gabe Macky, our senior homicide detective, who's lucky enough to keep working dead body cases while I'm stuck handling old men.

"I thought it was you who needed rescuing?" he replies with a laugh.

"Only from cat calls and devil cats." Gabe is aware of my current feline problem.

More laughter fills the line. "I'll take pity on you," he says between chuckles. "I cleared you with Sergeant Spence to take a case that was just called in. He thinks you've paid your dues out of homicide and he's impressed you haven't had a complaint."

I can only snort. My exact words to Sergeant Spence when he told me I was reassigned to property crimes were, "I've paid my dues and don't deserve this." He laughed and told me I was the rookie homicide detective and would continue paying my dues. I have no real reason to complain but it wouldn't be me if I didn't. The last thing I want to do is disappoint my supervisor.

"My escapades this morning could change his no complaint clause," I say with glee. "I put Jeb Garland in his place and did it in front of his cronies." I hear Gabe's groan and my lips curl into another smile. "We'll make a deal; you get me out of my current assignment and I'll cook your favorite meal." The stress I've felt this past week lightens. No one wants dead bodies, but working petty crimes is worse than boring. Not that shooting through a store window is petty because it isn't. I just need a challenge and harassing old men is not a life goal of mine.

"Hopefully, your run-in with Jeb

won't put you back in hot water with the sergeant. The case I'm on needs legwork and I can't manage the new one right now. Take down this info and call the hospital as soon as you can."

"Got it," I say after writing down my victim's name and the doctor's information.

I hang up and glance into the rearview mirror at Bell. "We're off the hook and you won't need to take a bite out of any old men."

She barks so I know we're on the same page.

CHAPTER TWO

After getting situated in my office, I call Mountain General Hospital and ask to speak with Doctor Timmons who I'm unfamiliar with. I'm placed on hold while Bell gets comfortable on her bed in the corner and I play a game of solitaire on my computer. Nauseating organ music also fills my ear.

Finally, a gruff voice interrupts the blazing concerto of horror. "Dr. Timmons," he says.

"This is Detective Jolett. I'm contacting you about Melony Chaplin, a patient admitted last night."

He sighs heavily. "Hello Detective, I was expecting your call. Ms. Chaplin is critical and unresponsive to vasopressors. I was just reviewing her condition with a specialist in New York. So far, her bloodwork has come back negative for known toxins but Dr. Eagan and I believe I'm dealing with a poison of some sort. I'm reaching out to toxicologist specialists to see if they have ideas for treatment. I spoke with Ms. Chaplin's mother on the phone earlier and she told me her daughter has been in a safe house for several months. She's also concerned about the ex-son-in-law who's threatened her daughter many times. One of the threats concerned poison which helped lead me to my current avenue of treatment and possible causes for my patient's condition."

I write down the word "vasopressors" to look up after I'm off the phone. I learned early as a detective that most doctors speak a foreign language and have no idea they are doing it. If I let him know I'm not medically hip, his explanations will change and I can lose vital data. "If Ms. Chaplin is unable to answer my questions, I'll need her mother's information." I also don't need to offer sympathy to the doctor because it's his job just like investigations are my job. Sympathy gets us nowhere and his time is just as valuable as mine.

"Her mother told me she phoned Ms. Chaplin yesterday evening and her voice was slurred along with having hallucinations. The mother called an ambulance. By the time they arrived, Ms. Chaplin was unresponsive and has remained so. The most important thing at this point is finding the cause of her condition. I'm not saying conclusively that it's poisoning but I'm running out of other scenarios."

The doctor goes into more detail about serology and other aspects of dealing with poisons and I'm promptly lost and scribbling furiously in my notebook. I give the appropriate responses because he finally gives me the mother's information. I tell him I will be in touch and end the call.

After the doctor mentioned the safe house, a lightbulb went off in my head that led me to run Melony's name through our police department database. I go straight to the report I wrote years ago while covering shift for a patrol officer.

Victim: Melony Chaplin
Suspect: Beau Chaplin

Beau's name rings a bell and more lightbulbs go off as I read the entire report. Beau likes to use his fists and threaten death. When I interviewed Melony, she told me about the many times he threatened to kill her. She didn't mention poison to me but she did mention additional dangerous behavior such as locking her in the closet for hours without food or water. Beau took a plea deal, served a month in jail, and went on about his life. At the time, I doubted Melony would leave him but I guess I was wrong.

I dial Melony's mother.

"Hello."

"Mrs. Rogers, this is Detective Jolett. I was hoping to speak with you about your daughter's medical condition."

"Thank you, Detective. I've been waiting to speak with someone who might be able to help. I know Beau did something." She sniffs softly and I give her time to collect herself. "I just know he poisoned her."

Knowing something and proving it are two different things. "I need to understand her relationship with her ex," I say. "I've read the report on a domestic I had involving them years ago but your perspective would be helpful. Please start at the beginning if you can."

"Thank you and please call me Marge," she requests. "The abuse started shortly after they married but my daughter didn't tell me about it for several years." Her voice holds anger and frustration. "I knew something was wrong because she mostly stopped talking to me and things didn't add up. My daughter wouldn't show up for family events and had sketchy reasons. I finally surprised her at home while Beau was at work. That was the first time I saw the results of his fists on her poor face. She still wouldn't say a lot so I did my own digging and discovered he was arrested several times for hurting her. The last time he beat her, she agreed to find help and ended up in the safe house. I was so proud of her." Her voice goes quiet and she sniffs a few more times.

"Mrs. Rogers, Marge," I correct.

"I'm sorry," she repeats. "This is so hard. I should have been there for her from the beginning. I thought she would grow stronger once she was away from him but she started avoiding my calls and I suspected they were back together. When I spoke to her last night, she was talking crazy and her words were slurred."

"What did she say that seemed crazy?" I ask.

"She said the clothes didn't fit and they should have and she thought they weren't hers. I asked what clothes she was talking about and she started saying something else about the kitchen and it being all wrong. I thought she was drunk or high on drugs and neither is something I've known my daughter to do. I hung up and called an ambulance." She sniffs again. "They told me I possibly saved her life."

"The doctor mentioned his conversation with you and that you're worried poison could be involved. Why is that?"

"It was something my daughter said after she moved into the safe house. She told me she lived in fear he would poison her and it was something he threatened many times."

I find this strange. Poison is something women use, rarely men. "Did she mention a specific poison?" I must ask even though I'm sure Marge would have mentioned it to the doctor.

"No. The doctor asked that too but I never thought it could happen and I didn't dig deeper. It sounded ridiculous at the time and now I know better."

"Do you know where Beau is at this moment? Does he have a job?"

"Yes, he works at the tomato plant Monday through Friday."

The local tomato plant employs men and women from the county jail while they're incarcerated. If you work hard and need a job after serving time, the tomato plant will hire you. The plant is located about five miles outside city limits in a remote area between us and the next town south. The sheriff's department has jurisdiction if the crime happened there but the safe house Melony is in lands the case in my backyard. Unless he poisoned her outside the city limits, if he poisoned her, jurisdiction won't be in question. I'm not convinced

Melony was poisoned but like the doctor, I won't count it out.

"Do you know where her cell phone is?" If she's been in contact with Beau, her phone will have the details. The phone records will also tell me a lot. Cell phones have become paramount to most investigations these days and the minicomputers hold a person's life.

"I don't think the ambulance crew brought it and I haven't been to her house," Marge answers.

"It would be better to stay away until we know for sure what's happened to your daughter. I'm giving you my phone number in case you think of something involving her case." I read off the number and tell her I will call back if I discover anything of importance. She also gives me Melony's cell number so I can start the process of obtaining a warrant for her phone records.

After hanging up, I run the number through an internet search to find her provider and then fax a hold order to the company. They place a hold on her text messages, voicemail, and call records for the previous 180 days. A year ago, I could simply have called the County Attorney's Office and asked them to fax a subpoena but case law changed and now a warrant is needed. I don't yet have enough evidence that a crime has been committed but I need my ducks in a row if things line up accordingly.

I check the clock.

It's better to approach Beau after he leaves work. The plant lets out at four p.m., giving me time to kill. I decide to work with Bell and update her K9 training book. Before I gather her toys, Officer Leo Franks sticks his head inside my office. He hasn't shaved in the past few hours and he sports a five-o'clock shadow. It only accents his Italian heritage in the best possible way. He reminds me of the brother I never had.

"I hear you're back on homicide," he says without preamble.

I nod. "News travels fast."

"It does when I'm given the stray bullet case," he replies grumpily and even goes so far as to give me his pouty face.

I bite my lip to keep from laughing at his three-year-old antics. "You have five leads," I say with a straight face. "The problem is any one of them could die of old age before they're interviewed. I strongly urge you to notify the gang task force and have their group gang identified first. They all wear suspenders, baseball caps, and exude the smell of Fixodent." I keep my expression bland even though I know he reads the hilarity in my eyes.

"Are you done?" he asks in a testy voice a normal person would heed.

I, of course, have Bell to protect me from surly officers and have no intention of stopping my comedic routine.

"Thank you, yes, I'm done with the entire case and gladly hand it off to your excellent police old man expertise. If Jeb Garland cat whistles your way, please let me know so I can sic Bell on him. I don't like threatening old men so it would be great if I can back up the threats I made."

Leo rolls his eyes. "Forward what you have and I'll handle Jeb Garland along with the salty old men who run in his gang."

"If you gang identify them, the person responsible could get a life sentence." My voice is singsong sweet. "Even thirty days for someone that old could amount to death by lethal food in our jail."

Leo does a sudden about-face and walks out with my laughter floating behind him.

"Wow," I tell Bell. "Someone left their good mood at home. This would only be better if Conners got the case. I would have a field day and I would also take home all the blue ribbons for effort. Leo won't be nearly as fun to tease."

Bell blinks a few times, then closes her eyes again. Lazy is at an end when I pull her toybox from the shelf. Her eyes pop open and she jumps to her feet with her tail going a hundred miles an hour. There's nothing like sniffing out explosives to get the blood pumping in her K9 body.

CHAPTER THREE

I don't like approaching Beau Chaplin without Bell. I also know she can be intimidating and she won't help get the information I want from this interview. I need to lock Beau into a story and then uncover the truth. People lie because they have something to hide. Melony has a current restraining order against Beau. He shouldn't have had contact with her at all. I'll find out regardless of what he tells me but this first interview is crucial.

After leaving a sad-faced Bell in my office, I park down the street from Beau's house. It's a blue, at one point, run-down one-story that hasn't seen maintenance in a decade. Even the trees out front have died and show hope of becoming petrified wood. What makes the picture absolutely perfect is the broken toilet resting about five feet from the front door. I know there's a toilet display in every city in America but we seem to have more than our fair share here in town and they always strike me as hideous. I don't exactly enjoy trips to our city dump but to keep a broken toilet from decorating my yard, I would make the sacrifice.

Beau is dropped off within fifteen minutes of my arrival. My car is unmarked and neither man looked my direction when they drove past. I only realize it's Beau when he steps from the car. I jot down the license plate. The person dropping him off is gone within seconds of Beau climbing from the vehicle. I give Beau time to walk inside his front door before I exit my car and jog over. Beau, who barely closed the door, opens it immediately at my knock. His jovial expression changes as soon as he recognizes me.

He's a short, wiry man with brown hair that's a little too long and sticks out from the sides of his ballcap. He's not my idea of good-looking but at some point, Melony must have been attracted to something about him. I do, however, remember his sour expression well. Men like Beau do not like female cops arresting them. It upsets their personal sense of justice that allows them to beat up women. Our last encounter was years ago; Beau's anger remains a steady burn. He'll never forget me. Joy sings sweetly through my veins at the thought.

"I need to speak with you about your ex-wife, Melony," I say before he slams the door in my face. My recorder is in my pocket, picking up our voices to help me write my report after this front porch interview.

"I have nothing to say to you," he snaps.

"That's your statement?" I allow the last of the sentence to drop off in tone, like I'm incredulous.

"What do you mean statement?" he demands while puffing up his chest and standing taller. To me he looks like an inflatable outdoor Christmas decoration that's only half full of air.

"Your ex-wife is in the hospital and I need to ask you a few questions. If your one and only statement is 'I have nothing to say to you,' I'm good with it." I take a step back and turn slightly.

"Why would I have anything to do with her being in critical condition?" he rushes to say before I leave. His tone reflects his worry about himself and has nothing to do with Melony's condition. Or at least that's my opinion.

I don't smile or give away what his attitude does for my cold dead heart. I never mentioned Melony was in critical condition and Beau doesn't seem the least surprised or upset that she's in the hospital. We live in a small community and news travels fast so I don't consider this a solid clue. Yet. It will be because I can feel the animosity he has for his ex-wife. He's filled with hatred toward women in general, but Melony is his primary focus. He also thinks he's smarter than all women. It's the downfall of most abusers.

"My questions are quick and simple," I tell him sweetly. "It's up to you whether you answer or not." The wheels in his head turn while he considers what will be best for him. It's never an easy decision and I have nowhere to be and have no intention of hurrying him along.

He shuffles his feet a few times. "Ask but I'm not saying I'll answer," he says petulantly. I almost expect him to drop down and punch his fists into the ground in a temper tantrum. It literally wouldn't surprise me. Or maybe kick the toilet. I hold these thoughts back.

"Do you know if your ex has any allergies the doctor should be aware of?" This question is simply to keep him off-balance. He falls for it.

His face scrunches slightly while he thinks, thus taking his mind off the next lie he plans to tell me. "She's allergic to some medication the doctor gave her years ago for an infection but I don't know what it's called."

"Thank you, that helps," I assure him. "Does she have any enemies that you know of?" This is also meant to throw him off.

"No," he answers quickly.

"When was the last time you saw her?" I say this immediately after his previous answer, giving him no time to gather his thoughts.

He shuffles his feet again. "It's been months but I don't know the date. Is that all you have for me?"

"Not at all." I smile and continue. "Were you aware she's in the hospital?"

His eyes become laser pinpoints and his voice goes icy. "You just told me."

"Thank you, that's all I have." I give him a satisfied smile and walk away. The hairs on the back of my neck go up but I refuse to turn and look. The door doesn't close behind him and I feel him watching. I don't even turn when I'm in my car and driving away. It goes against my training but sometimes it's a necessity. A detective's and a police officer's jobs are quite different. I can't always watch my back and current funding means detectives don't ride together. I live with it because we have no choice.

Bell lifts her head and thumps her tail against her bed when I enter my office. She climbs to her feet and stretches her front legs and then the back ones with the grace of a leopard. "Come on, I'll take you outside for a break," I tell her, using my guilty mom voice. She wags her tail even more and licks my hand. And, just like that, I'm forgiven for leaving her behind.

It's my rotten luck that Officer Stanly Conners pulls into the parking lot as soon as Bell and I are outside. We've butted heads since I started at the department. His father sits on the city council and it gives Stanly a sense of importance. Most importantly for the department, his father hasn't cracked what's needed to get his son in a detective or supervisory position. With the unfriendly looks Stanly usually gives me, you would think I was singlehandedly responsible for his inability to promote. Someone should break the news that it's all on him. His superiority complex does not endear him to the department or the town regardless of who daddy is.

Today Stanly has an agenda because he walks straight for me. Why am I so lucky? "If you accidently bite him, I'll look the other way," I whisper to Bell.

She stays at perfect attention and doesn't leave my side even without the leash. She isn't fond of Stanly either.

"I hear you're back on homicide detail," he says from a few feet away. He's in uniform. It's his face and attitude that grates on my nerves. Okay, the fact he wears a uniform and has a badge also grates. He's in his thirties and has been a cop for over ten years. He wears dark sunglasses no matter the time of day or night. At some point, someone must have told him they were cool. That person was an idiot because the glasses are so far past cool that they've fermented. He always has a phony grin and loves displaying his perfectly capped teeth with his not so cute dimples. Someone told me he lost a tooth in a fight early in his career and had them all capped. He works out and thinks he's a gift to women everywhere. I dislike him so much; I grind my less than perfect teeth whenever he's around.

Conners won't approach closer with Bell next to me. His favorite tactic is stepping into my personal space much like I did to Jeb earlier today. Bell, and Suii before her, cured Conners' bad habit, at least when he's dealing with me.

Leo might have given me a hard time with my case being pawned off on him but

I knew he was joking. I've learned Stanly wraps his jokes in threats and insinuations that are not a joke. So, I don't answer the question immediately.

After a few beats, I pleasantly say, "Bell needs to do her business. She's a little upset over me leaving her for the afternoon so don't make any sudden moves."

"Release," I tell Bell. I'm also full of crap about sudden moves. It's bad of me to pull Conners' chain but I can't seem to help myself.

Stanly raises his arms slightly and rests his hands on his duty belt. It wouldn't stop Bell from grabbing him if she wanted to but it makes me happy that he sees her as the threat she is.

I give Stanly my full attention as soon as Bell trots to her favorite section of weeds that pass for grass in the great State of Arizona.

I shrug. "Homicide needs me, I guess." I'm curious about what he's up to so I hold back a snide reply.

Conners smirks which he thinks passes as a smile. "There's a rumor that DJ's applying at another agency and there may be a detective position opening."

That tells me all I need to know. He wants to sweet-talk me in the hope I'll put in a good word. Last time I checked, Satan had not frozen over his dominion and there's absolutely no chance of me praising Conners to anyone, for anything.

"DJ is a good detective and I would hate to lose him." I'm giving Stanly absolutely zero wiggle room.

He puffs his chest out much like Beau did earlier. It's sad that I dislike one of my co-workers as much as I dislike a wife beater. I also know I had a chip on my shoulder for a long time and the entire department watched their step around me. I'm not proud of it. I'm also not a narcissistic idiot like Stanly. I changed. He never will.

He smiles graciously unless you notice the burn in his eyes that says the dislike is mutual. "Just thought I would give you a heads-up that I'll be moving into the detective division. Macky will retire in the next few years and I have my eyes on homicide. I think we would work well together."

I need to vomit but I don't want to soil my shoes. "Best of luck with the detective position if DJ leaves." I glance at Bell who is now sniffing along the fence. "Come on, girl. It's time to go home." Bell runs to the back of my vehicle and waits on me.

"I know I'll make a better partner than your dog. You have my promise on that," Stanly says to get the last word in.

His jibe stops me and I give him my full attention. I add my own fake smile to match his. "I wouldn't count on that. Bell has four shoes to fill and you can only try to fill two." I laugh like I'm joking. Both of us know this conversation is not congenial.

After Bell is loaded in my vehicle, I climb into the driver's seat, close the door, and call Gabe. I barely give him a chance to answer. "If you retire in the next few years, I will never buy you a Christmas present again."

He laughs. "Since you've never bought me a Christmas present, I'll assume your favorite officer cornered you like he did me."

"Did you tell him you planned to retire in the next few years?" I demand crossly.

His laughter goes up a notch. "No, but he hinted I should."

"Well, don't," I say and hang up. I crank my neck around and glare at Bell. "If I'm ever forced to work with that jerk, you will have free rein to bite him every other day. When you aren't doing your thing, I'll be punching him in the face. One way or another, he won't be welcome."

Bell doesn't so much as whine. She must be too busy thinking of ways to turn Stanly Conners into dog food.

CHAPTER FOUR

at Cat is pacing at his front door when we pull up. Bell growls through the window, threatening his life. Rat Cat swishes his tail in spite and ignores us. I practically drag Bell, who is trained better than this, through my front door. She fights me the entire way.

I'm always looking for an excuse to call Jack at the K9 division in Phoenix. A dog set on eating the neighbor's cat is a good reason, right?

"K9s are Us, at your service," Jack answers. He obviously knows it's me and my heart gives a small flutter. Leo, with all his good looks, does nothing for me. Jack, on the other hand, makes me wonder what it would be like to have someone to talk to just for the sake of talking. It's a strange reaction for me to have. Jack and I live in different worlds and neither wants a change. This defines our relationship. Why take the next step if it won't get us anywhere?

"We have a cat situation and Bell isn't handling it well."

"I'm with Bell. Cats have what's called dander and it makes everyone around them crazy."

"You made that up."

I enjoy his laughter and this time is no exception. "They do have dander and I'm allergic. If Bell has the good sense to dislike cats, I wouldn't worry about it."

"I don't like cats either," I assure him.

"Does this mean we have something in common?" I can still hear the merriment in his tone.

"Do you have any suggestions other than misplacing the cat on my next trip to the dump?"

"Drastic times call for drastic measures. I have a special ops friend who handles these types of situations for a fee. He could possibly help you and there would be no evidence left behind. I think my friend is a sociopath but that's beside the point."

"Now I'm unsure if you're joking or not."

He laughs with more gruffness in his voice and it sounds really good. "We're talking about cats. Nothing is off the table, even potential serial killers," he replies.

"I'll remember to never make you sneeze," I answer. This conversation isn't going anywhere and I feel sad that I have nothing to keep him on the line. Pathetic, thy name is Laci.

"You do that. They say an allergy can start at any time."

I give this entire dialogue thing one more try. "I'm back on homicide and may be investigating a missing cat case soon. It could really mess up my eighty-five percent case clearance rate if I protect Bell and don't turn her in."

"Bell's tough and can take the heat. Congratulations on your reassignment. Working the trenches of the lower echelon of detectives was probably quite hard on you."

"An old man whistled at me."

"The nerve. Did Bell attack?"

I rest my hip against the kitchen counter. "He wasn't a cat so the old man was safe."

"And we're back to cats," he says warmly.

"It's an ugly cat." Bell whines for her dinner but it's at the perfect time. "See, Bell agrees."

"Even kittens are ugly," Jack replies earnestly.

"Now you've gone too far. A man should be ashamed for not liking kittens." I think we're flirting but who knows. We talk dogs and now cats. It's kind of becoming our thing.

"I hate to cut this short but I have a date," he says abruptly. My heart drops and all I can do is swallow before he continues. "His Majesty is having trouble and I brought him home. It's a training date."

"His majesty?" I ask now that I can breathe again.

"It's his name, capital H, capital M, and no, he didn't get it from me. He's a Belgian

Malinois and he needs a little extra work. He's an explosives dog like Bell without the good disposition."

"I'm sure you'll find him the perfect partner."

His voice turns wistful. "Actually, if I could afford him, he'd be mine."

I never asked why Jack didn't have a dog. "It must be rough to give them up when it's time for them to go to a new owner," I say as I push off the counter to make Bell's dinner.

"Some are harder than others."

I place Bell's bowl on the floor and start searching the refrigerator for myself. "If you need a shoulder to cry on, after he finds his forever home, give me a call. You were there for me." I wouldn't have made it through Suii's death if it weren't for Jack.

"It's a deal. Call me if the cat situation gets worse and I'll drive down and save the day with my rifle."

"You're all heart."

"We're talking cats."

"I'm not disagreeing."

Our call ends with me smiling. Maybe

when we're old and gray and both retired, things could work out for us. Until then, Jack is a good friend and I'm glad I have him in my corner.

I pop a frozen dinner into the microwave and tell myself it says it's healthy on the outside of the package so it must be healthy. I eat in front of the evening news, then do a load of laundry while Bell goes out back and inspects the yard. I walk out when she starts barking. Of course, Rat Cat is sitting on his throne and casually cleaning himself without a care in the world.

"Come inside, Bell. He's got your number and you're letting him win."

Bell follows reluctantly.

It's a hard life when a K9 has a feline nemesis. Kind of like Conners. Shooting him is simply a bad idea.

The following day begins with me running interference between Rat Cat and Bell again. Once we go through our new morning ritual and reach my office, I call Dr.

Timmons for an update on Melony.

"I've forwarded her tests and blood-work to the doctor in New York and he's sharing it with his colleagues. I've checked everything from toxic shock to known poisons and I'm coming up empty. Her liver and kidneys are shutting down and her vitals aren't good but she's still alive for now. I also had my nurse call EMS and check on the ambulance crew. None have complained of unusual symptoms after picking her up and being inside her home. If it is poison, I have no idea what I'm looking for or how it got into her system."

The call ends shortly after that. Melony is still alive and I hope she stays that way. I pull out my recorder to begin typing my initial report. I also run Beau's vital statistics through the Department of Transportation records and find a vehicle registered to him. It was most likely sitting in the garage when I was at his place. Access to a vehicle makes it easier to have access to Melony.

I need to look inside her home and the only way I can do that is with a warrant. I also need to speak with someone in the

State's Hazardous Materials Emergency Response Division. It takes me a few minutes to locate the business card from one of their guys I took special training from.

Investigator Wilson answers on the second ring. "Hi, this is Detective Jolett. I took a hazmat class you instructed and I'm taking you up on your offer of a phone call and questions if you have time?"

"Of course, what do you have for me, Detective Jolett?"

I give him minimal information which is basically all I have. "I doubt I could get a search warrant at this point but I need to know if I should enter the home if I do get one."

"Absolutely not. Our special hazmat unit will clear the home for you first. From the symptoms you've given me, there are several poisons you could be dealing with but they're common and her doctor would have those off the list at this point. If there is poison, it's most likely something easy to obtain even if scarce. Internet records would be your best bet. These clowns like to research and come up with the perfect murder. Most of the time, their trail is a mile long."

"I'll be running down the story he gave me. If I can prove he's had contact with her, I think I can get the warrant. Since she was in a safe house, it gives me a little more meat for the judge."

"I'll send a list of uncommon poisons that aren't prevalent online. You can pass them on to the doctor."

"Thank you for your help and if I can get inside the home, I'll take you up on the offer for hazmat."

Our conversation ends and I'm back at the drawing board. I lift the phone and dial Melony's mother.

"I'm looking for names of Melony's friends. If she was seeing Beau, she might have told one of them."

"Her best and really only friend is Stephanie Eaton. Beau kept my daughter isolated when they were together but Stephanie hung in there. Let me grab her number for you."

I wait a minute before she comes back on the line and gives me the number. Our call ends and Stephanie answers on the first ring. "Hello."

"This is Detective Jolett. I'm calling about Melony Chaplin. Her mother gave me your name and number."

"That jerk poisoned her, didn't he?" From the sound of her voice, Beau has an enemy.

"I haven't determined that but I am investigating her condition. Anything you can tell me would help."

"I know she was seeing him. She started acting strange about a month ago," she insists passionately. "I asked her specifically if she was dating the jerk again and she wouldn't answer. That's a yes in my book. I told her if he came into Lamar's, I would smash him over the head with whatever bottle is in my hand. I'm a bartender there and I know I shouldn't say this to a cop, but I still plan to keep that promise."

"No, you shouldn't say that to a cop," I tell her honestly. "Did she mention a phone call from him, or any other type of contact?"

"She came by the bar on weeknights and had dinner with me except for Tuesdays. On Tuesdays she had a standing date with her mom. Marge told me Melony hadn't been to a Tuesday dinner in over a month. If she wasn't with me or with her mom, there's only one explanation and she had to be meeting Beau."

"Thank you, that helps." It really did. I have no doubt that Melony was seeing her ex. "Do you know what color Beau's car is?" The vehicle's color was not in the DMV information.

"Yes, it's an ugly green with the paint falling off."

"Thank you, if you think of anything, please call me."

"Is Melony going to make it?" Her voice is minus the anger now and she's close to tears.

"I don't know," I say truthfully.

Our conversation is over but she speaks again before I hang up. "If Beau hurt her, you won't find his body."

"That's also something you shouldn't say to a cop."

"Find the evidence you need and lock him up so I can't get to him."

"Noted," I say and hang up.

I walk over to Bell and scratch her head. "We all need friends like that. I have you and Melony has Stephanie."

Bell covers my hand in dog slobber as her way of letting me know she agrees.

CHAPTER FIVE

My first break comes after I check out the location of the safe house. It just so happens that Lucky Gas is around the corner. Like many safe houses in small rural communities, everyone including the abuser is aware of the house's location. In extremely dangerous circumstances, the case worker will get the victim out of town. It's hard because funds aren't readily available and they must pick and choose who needs escape the worst. Melony wasn't lucky.

The safe house is white stucco with a red door. I take pictures in case I go after a warrant and need the precise description. After I'm sure I have what I need, I head to Lucky Gas and Wash.

The owner, Larry, greets me. He's in

his seventies but doesn't look a day over sixty-nine. He's a large man with an equally large smile. Sad that someone would attack his store. He's known to help people in need and until a month ago hadn't raised his price on a cup of coffee in over ten years.

"I heard you put the dust on old Jeb," he says with a twinkle in his eyes. "Wish I could have seen it. Do you think he's the one who shot my window?"

"He fits the profile of an old lecher but I'm not sure about the bullet hole. Officer Franks is taking over the investigation and will come by and speak to you in the next day or so."

"He already showed up and I told him what I told you. The coffee gaggle is filled with a bunch of mean old men who married mean old ladies. Any one of them could be responsible. They're still buying my coffee at the higher price, though."

"If you raise the price again, you might get rid of them for good."

"And ruin all the gossip they share?" He chuckles. "Not a chance."

I laugh. "I'm actually here to spend

some quality time with your video system. It could help with my latest case."

"I haven't heard of any homicides recently?" He poses it as a question. Larry is also a gossip hound.

"Hopefully, you won't. Mind if I have a look?" Anything I say will be spread around town in under five minutes.

"Be my guest," he says and turns to a customer who walks in, saving me from further small talk.

I head to the back of the store and then up a built-in ladder to the loft where the equipment is stored. Whoever shot into the store did it out of camera range. It's another reason the coffee gaggle was on my suspect list. Teens wouldn't know about the camera system or how far to stay back when shooting the window.

I've used Lucky's equipment to check tape quite a few times and I know how this specific machinery works. My first check is last Tuesday starting at four p.m. after Beau gets off work. I have the tape running at high speed. Within a minute, I spot Beau's friend's car with them both inside, heading home from work. I slow the footage and watch them drive past Lucky's without turning down Melony's street.

I run through the next hour and then the next at high speed without seeing a sign of Beau. I then switch to a slower rate and try again. At 5:25, I spot the faded-green Mazda. Even on the small screen I can see where the paint is chipping away. Beau is driving and no one else is in the car. He turns down Melony's street and I lose sight of him.

"Thank goodness," I say to myself as I head out.

Bell waits for me patiently in the back of the vehicle and I give her my next move once I pull away from the gas station. "It's time to hit the neighbors and ask about a green Mazda."

Bell sighs and hunkers down in the back. I'm thinking she's aware it's not something she'll be helping with. Where's a good bomb threat when you need one?

No one is home at the first door I knock on, so I go to the neighbor on the east side of the safe house. An older woman answers. She's somewhere past seventy, about five feet tall, and from the gym clothes she's wearing, black leggings with a tight shirt that says, "If it jiggles, it's available," she's spunky.

"Have you noticed an older model green Mazda with peeling paint parked in front of your neighbor's house?" I ask after introducing myself.

"He doesn't park in front of Melony's place; he parks about five houses down across the street. I'm assuming he's a woman beater and he's been sneaking into the safe house?"

"You may have assumed correctly." I'm not dumb and lying to this woman will get me nowhere.

"Tuesday nights and sometimes on the weekend. I keep a close eye on that place."

"If I showed you a photo lineup, could you possibly identify him?"

"I could but I can also give you his name. My nephew works with him at the tomato plant and he told me who it was. The nephew had a drug problem a few years back but he's doing good now. You won't be looking for him anytime soon."

"A name would be great."

"It's Beau something. I can call my nephew and ask for his last name if you need it."

"Beau is fine. Could you call me if he shows up to the house again?" I hand her my card.

"If you could arrest him somewhere on this block and I could witness it, I'd be thankful. I do understand that might not work but it never hurts to put the thought in your head."

"It's there and I'll do my best, but no promises," I answer with a smile. She really is spunky.

It's hard not to skip back to my car after taking down her information. She was more than happy to go on the record as who reported seeing Beau at the safe house. He crossed the restraining order and I'll get my warrant. Now it's time to sit down and type.

Two hours later, my preliminary report is written along with the warrant. With fingers crossed that I find a judge in a good mood, I head to the courthouse. I bypass the justice of the peace and head upstairs to the superior court judge. He isn't available but John Eship, the Judge Pro Tempore, or pro tem judge as we say, is in his chambers and can see me.

John is in his forties with each brown hair perfectly in place and a suit collar beneath his black robe. His face is thin with large teeth and his smile is refreshing because he does it often. He practiced law in town before he took this appointment a few years ago. He also likes Bell which is in my favor today.

"How are you, Detective?" he asks when I enter his chambers. I allow Bell to walk over for her dose of judge love. He pets the scruff of her neck and then her chin. He owns large dogs and understands not to raise his hand above her head. Bell likes him too and I'm glad I brought her in with me. Not that Judge Eship will give me a warrant without cause. He won't. He will make sure my warrant is airtight and able to withstand scrutiny if I end up in trial. This said, it never hurts to grease the wheels with a little dog slobber.

"I'm doing well and as you can see, Bell is having a great day."

"She's a good dog. What can I help you with, Detective?"

"I have a warrant that needs a signature," I say and hand over the paperwork.

He flips through the pages quickly and stops at my probable cause statement to read slowly. He grabs glasses from his desk and puts them on. He grunts here and there before looking up. "I've had this gentleman in my courtroom several times. I sincerely hope your case isn't what it looks like." His head drops again and he reviews the warrant from the beginning, checking for errors that could possibly cause trouble.

I'm relieved because I know, at this point, he'll sign off. It takes the judge ten minutes to finish his review and hand the signed document back. "Have the court clerk stamp, date, and file, and you're good to go."

"Thank you, Your Honor," I say sincerely. The judge won't badmouth Beau in my presence. If this case goes to an arrest and he's the presiding judge, it could overturn a verdict if he's overheard dissing the suspect. The judge understands what I'm after and he agrees that Melony's house should be searched and that's all I ask.

I dial Investigator Wilson with hazmat and schedule a unit to go into the house first. They're meeting me there in the morning. I head back to the station to speak with my supervisor about having a rookie watch the house overnight.

Sergeant Spence is in his office doing his never-ending paperwork. I don't care how old I am; I never plan to take a supervisory position.

"How you doing, Bell?" he asks her while ignoring me. They do their friendship dance for a minute before he gives me his attention. "You owe me for putting you back in homicide," he states.

I'm surprised. "Was I being punished?"

This makes him laugh. "Teaming you with a K9 was punishment. Taking you off homicide while Detective Marin was out was necessity. I now find it more necessary for you to work homicide. I made the case to the chief for the other detectives to take up the slack and earn some overtime." He cocks his head. "You owe me."

I raise my hand, palm out. "I owe you and will repay my debt with honor, sir." I click my heels together three times like Dorothy from the *Wizard of Oz* and keep my spine straight.

Sergeant Spence looks at Bell. "How do you put up with her? She has no appreciation for authority and no manners at all." He glances at me again. "What's up?"

"I have a warrant for the safe house and hazmat is meeting me first thing tomorrow morning. I need a rookie watching the place all night to keep the integrity of my warrant."

He picks up the phone and relays the information to one of the officers.

It's time to head home and get some rest. Search warrants make for long days.

CHAPTER SIX

I'm dead to the world when Bell's low growl wakes me. She flies off the bed and runs for the front of the house. Groggily, I grab my gun from the bedside nightstand and follow without shoes or my phone. Bell's standing at her locked dog door with her hackles raised and a low growl rumbling from her throat. I flip on the back light and peek out the window.

Of course, it's the darn cat. He's eating something on my patio and I'm worried he caught a mouse and decided to use my porch as his dining table. Or a rat, I think after more bleary-eyed inspection. Something strange catches my eye and I open the back door after commanding Bell to stay.

Rat Cat lets out a long solid meow but stays put when I walk out. The cat looks at me, then goes back to what he was doing. My brain remains slow and it takes a moment to realize what I'm seeing. I move forward quickly and the cat finally backs off with a hiss. He jumps onto the brick wall and glares from above. I hunch down and examine the partially eaten meat. I grab Bell's water bowl, spill the contents, and scoop the meat into it. My hands are shaking.

The meat was tossed over my fence and there's only one reason.

Someone tried to poison Bell.

I wash my hands quickly, then call dispatch to have an officer sent to my house. Changing clothes with record speed, I place Bell on her lead and keep her next to me as I examine my backyard with a flashlight. The cat is gone and even though I'm not a fan, I hope he didn't ingest poisoning or glass or whatever the person placed in the meat. Part of Jack's K9 training was understanding that your dog is for your protection and also a liability when it comes to ways to hurt you.

I'm finding out exactly how true that is. My heartrate still hasn't returned to normal even after several minutes and my anger grows by the second. I impatiently wait for the officer's arrival with no recourse and it's driving me crazy.

With my current run of luck, Officer Conners is the responding officer, dark glasses and all. It's hard to hold a snarky remark back and it's only possible because I bite my lip. He remains his old cocky self until he examines the water dish and agrees with my assessment of the meat.

"Someone tried to poison your dog," he says in conclusion while shaking his head. He doesn't appear happy and it's a good reminder that we may infight but when an officer is in danger, we have each other's backs. Bell is an officer and Conners' displeasure is unmistakable.

"The case I'm working is quite possibly a poisoning. I don't believe in coincidence." I hate telling him anything about my current case but he's the responding officer and needs the details to take care of business or to pass it to a detective. I can't investigate this myself, unfortunately. It's possible we may need to pass it to another department. That's for Sergeant Spence to decide and I'm glad it's on his shoulders. I pat Bell's side and take a deep breath to calm my frayed nerves.

"Beau would do this," Conners says. "I've handled too many domestics at his place and I know what he's like."

I live nowhere near the safe house. The cameras located between Beau's place and mine click through my head. Before I can offer a suggestion, Conners offers the same thought. "I'll run his license and get a plate number, then check the cameras in town. If I can locate his vehicle near your vicinity, it gives me a little more circumstantial evidence."

He's been studying and knows all the big detective words now. "Thank you." I don't offer what I already have concerning Beau's plate number. These are two separate cases and Conners needs his own investigative trail. The words that leave my mouth next surprise even me. "I'll talk to Sergeant Spence about keeping you assigned to the case. Bell needs a hero right now and I'm a mess." This is truth and I don't mind admitting it. The possibility of losing Bell shakes me. "I need to pay my neighbors a visit so they can check on their cat," I say as my thoughts turn to the tabby. As much as he drives me crazy, I don't want him suffering.

"I'll bag the evidence and get it sent to the lab to determine what was used. Check your yard before allowing Bell outside. I'll have the officers cruise by more often until we have this settled."

"Thank you," I say again and the roof doesn't cave in. I'm actually grateful for his professionalism. He could be a great cop if he left his father's status behind and stopped pulling his usual crap.

After Conners collects his evidence and leaves, I walk to the neighbor's door and knock. It's four in the morning and Rat Cat hasn't returned to my yard. I'm really worried.

Bill answers the door with his wife Molly standing behind him. I've only spoken to them a handful of times and they've always been friendly. Right now, they're sleepy yet curious. I explain what's happened and say how sorry I am.

"The tabby cat?" asks Bill.

"Yes, I didn't know his name so I call him Rat Cat." Now I'm ashamed of the darn name. "He's sat on the fence between our backyards since you moved in."

"That's not our cat; we thought he was yours," Bill says in confusion.

I'm stumped. The cat showed up within days of Bill and Molly. "He paces in front of your door all the time. It never occurred to me he wasn't yours."

Bill looks over his shoulder at his wife who has a funny look on her face. "I feed him," she admits. "I thought he could use a little extra meat on his bones and I didn't think you fed him enough. That's why he's looking so much better now."

She must mean fat because that's what I see when looking at Rat Cat. "I've never fed him." I could have gotten rid of the darn pest weeks ago if I knew he didn't belong to my neighbors. "I'm really sorry to bother you. I'm going to grab Bell and we'll look for him. I don't want him suffering."

"We can help if you need," Bill offers. I can tell he really wants to go back to bed and

I let him off the hook.

"Bell and I have it covered. I truly am sorry for waking you."

They go back into the house and I fetch Bell. The next two hours are spent hunting for a cat who could be lying dead someplace. With a touch of sadness, I give up when it's time to prepare for my shift.

"Sorry, Bell," I say before jumping into the shower. "I don't think the cat will be back. I'll get this case solved and you'll have your dog door open again, I promise." For the time being, Bell will only go out after I check the yard. I'm in full agreement with Conners on this.

After drying my hair and dressing, Bell starts barking at the back door and I remove my gun from its holster to check what's up. Like every other morning, Rat Cat is at his place on the wall, looking like a king. It's stupid that I'm relieved. Still, never will I like cats and that's a promise.

"Come on, Bell," I say after she does her business and goes back to barking at the cat. "We have a criminal to catch. I think he's a serial poisoner and we need to put him out of business before someone dies."

Bell's on the same page and eagerly follows me to the car, leaving behind her furry and alive antagonist.

CHAPTER SEVEN

We're out early and I have an hour before I meet the hazmat unit at Melony's house. We travel past the police department as I drive out of town. I need to speak with someone at the tomato plant and see what kind of employee Beau is. If possible, I plan to slip in a few other questions while I'm at it.

About five miles from town, I take the turn that leads to the plant. It's set back about a quarter mile from the road. It's a sprawling place on about a hundred acres. I park and head inside leaving Bell sulking in her backseat. Okay, she doesn't sulk but her huff when she laid down let me know she wasn't happy to wait inside.

Mr. Dapple, the senior supervisor,

walks into the front office where I'm waiting and agrees to speak with me. He's somewhere in his sixties, wearing a beige jumpsuit with the arm sleeves rolled up. He catches me inspecting his prison tats and stretches his right arm out, pointing to the kindergarten-like blue-inked drawing of a mermaid or at least I think it's a mermaid. "This was my first. I did ten years in Perryville and accumulated most of my art while doing time."

I don't laugh at his use of the word art. He's proud of his tattoos. I also don't ask what he went away for. It's disrespectful and I need him on my side if that's even possible. "Did you work the tomato farm during your time?" I ask instead.

"Nah, Perryville's too far away. I worked a seasonal corn farm when I wasn't in trouble. Learned a lot about olericulture and found my calling. After moving up here, the tomato plant found me and it's been a good partnership."

"Olericulture?" I wasn't even sure if I said it correctly.

"It's everything from growing vegetables to marketing them. I enjoy working the entire process." He invites me to his office and I follow him out a side door, through a narrow outdoor alley, and into a small trailer. It has a low-slung brown couch and desk with a computer. I take the couch and it swallows me. If I need to get up quickly, I'll roll to the floor in order to get my feet beneath me. It will not be pretty. I give my full attention to Mr. Dapple.

"I would like to ask you about one of your employees. I'm trying to determine if he's a suspect or not and any light you cast would be valuable. Things like attendance and overall performance," I say before he can object. "It would be great if I could remove him from my suspect list."

And it would. I'm not lying. The best outcome here would be to find out Melony has some unidentified disease or virus and will eventually recover.

Dapple stares at me, judging if I'm a cop he can talk to. I've been in this situation before and I never know what I'll get with someone who did time. It always surprises me when they decide to talk. Mr. Dapple is one of my surprises.

"Give me a name and I'll help if I can," he finally agrees.

"Beau Chaplin," I offer without delay.

"Beau?"

"Yes, he's on my list. I would like to know his general work demeanor."

Mr. Dapple scratches his white-bearded chin in thought. "Beau's a good employee. He shows up on time and doesn't call in sick. He's gaining more responsibility and if he stays, he'll climb our ranks even faster. He's one of my best employees."

"I'm relieved, thank you." I add a smile to help him along. "What about his job description? What type of work does he do for you?"

I watch his shoulders relax and he leans back more fully in his chair. "Beau is currently working with our agriculture pest control specialist and like me, he may have found his calling. People want to buy organic now and we've been doing a lot of work to add hydroponics to our plant and give the people what they want. Eventually we will be a one-hundred-percent organic facility. The actual transition will take years and I see Beau as a key part to our success."

"What exactly does his job entail?"

"We use pesticides to control the pests that can and will destroy our crops. We also offer an education program. Beau wanted a job where he could learn and possibly go back to school and gain a degree. Agriculture pest control specialists make good money. Especially those who transition to organic and understand the changing need for non-pesticide solutions. I'm really pushing him to that end of things."

I nod my head and give a false relieved smile. "What about confrontation with other employees?" I decide to soften the question a bit. I actually have what I need and don't want Dapple suspicious. "I would basically like to know if Beau gets along with his coworkers."

"Absolutely, I've never had a complaint. He's liked and respected here and takes inmates under his wing as a mentor. For some of our workers, due to their criminal past or even present incarceration, they've never had a job where they're respected. We hire felons and give them a second chance. Workers like Beau are exactly who we're striving to help. When we help one, they in turn, help others. Besides putting out the best crop of tomatoes we can, helping those incarcerated is our goal."

My smile grows and I stand and place my hand out. Dapple stands and shakes my hand without thought. "Thank you," I say sincerely. "You've relieved my mind. You've also taught me a lesson today."

He smiles now and all concern leaves his expression. "How so?"

"My job has been to find the guilty and lock them up. Officers rarely think about what comes after someone serves their time. This company provides a service and I'm glad you're here." Maybe I'm going a bit overboard in my praise, but Dapple doesn't seem to think so and I'm being honest. We say our goodbyes as he walks me back to the front office.

Bell gives a small yip when I sit behind the wheel which tells me she needs a break. I pull over a short distance from the plant and let her out of the back. She's quick and I have just enough time to drop her at the police department before heading to Melony's house. If there is poison in the home, I want Bell nowhere near it.

The rookie officer who pulled the house-sitting duty is waiting for me along with a white hazmat van.

Two men and a woman step away from the rookie and greet me. We shake and I wave off the rookie before I explain what I learned at the tomato plant.

Investigator Lott, who oversees the hazmat unit, nods. "If he has access to ordering, there's a wide variety of chemicals he would be able to get his hands on. Our equipment checks for quite a few of them. We'll scan the house to make sure you can enter. Have you been inside at all?"

"No." I rub my hands together. "I want it safe, first."

"We are more than willing to gear you up and take you inside with us."

This is not something I considered but I'm game. First, I hand over my warrant and let him read it so we're all on the same page. He nods and hands it back when he's satisfied.

Gearing me up consists of a white hazmat suit, booties, gloves, and duct tape. They secure a small oxygen tank over my shoulder and attach it to a hood piece with a see-through face area. I feel like I have a part in a Hollywood virus movie.

Unfortunately, there's no one around to take video of me to show off to Gabe. He would get a kick out the gown and watching me walk like a zombie. I'm warned to keep an eye on my surroundings once we're inside and to stay away from sharp objects so I don't tear my suit.

Once the four of us are gowned and checked, I follow the hazmat crew inside. I bring my camera to take pictures and start snapping outside the door to capture the address to verify the address of my warrant.

Sound is muffled and even with the oxygen, I feel like I'm slowly suffocating. I slow my breathing and within a few seconds, collect myself. I snap more pictures after entering a small foyer. Lowering the camera, I check out the inside. I've been here several times through the years and it always looks different. I have the feeling each woman puts her touch on the place and leaves the changes behind when they go. Or maybe there's another explanation; I just don't know what it is.

"Stick by Sam while he scans each room," Investigator Lott tells me and points to the man wielding the device that registers toxins. The machine is a rectangular electronic box of some sort with a long metal wand attached to another smaller box. He places the wand to different surfaces and keeps an eye on a blinking green light on the machine.

Sam turns to me. "This is a gas chromatograph." He points to the larger machine in his hand. "And this is a mass spectrometer." He signals with the hand holding the long wand. If the light on the spectrometer turns red"—he points to the green blinking light—"a series of beeps will sound and we'll know what we have." He says this with a touch of excitement in his voice.

I've researched tons of poisons in the past twenty-four hours and I'm not as thrilled about finding something toxic as this guy, even while wearing my spacesuit. Thankfully, the light continues blinking green as we slowly make our way through the house.

Melony's bedroom is tidy like the rest of the place. I lived in different foster homes as a child and I hated when they were messy or in some cases filthy. I keep my condo clean and the easiest way to do it is not collecting junk. Melony is like me and lives a very minimalist lifestyle. Or maybe it's that this is a safe house and not a place of her own. I purchased my condo so I would have a home. The few items I have are important to me and now I have more dog junk than my own. Bell and I should really have a talk about her current collection of toys.

A loud continual beep pulls me from my thoughts. Sam sticks his head out of Melony's closet at the same time Investigator Lott and the woman walk in.

"The alert went off as soon as I entered the closet," Sam tells them. "I want to check the rest of the room before we proceed inside."

The woman, who introduced herself

as Carmen, carries a large test kit much like the kits we use to test for drugs. She lays the kit on the bed after Sam runs the probe over it. When no negative alerts are given, Sam heads back inside the closet.

"Things are about to get interesting," Investigator Lott says.

I watch what unfolds in fascination. Sam sticks his head out of the closet and tells Carmen he has a positive on several items. Carmen enters the closet. About two minutes later, she whistles. "We're dealing with paraquat," she says loudly.

Paraquat is one of the poisons available for farming, I recall. It's a weed killer.

"Color?" asks Lott.

"No dye. Came from outside the country," she replies.

"What does color have to do with it?" I ask.

Carmen walks out of the closet with a small vial of red fluid. "Paraquat is dyed blue so it's identifiable. It's also given a unique odor so poisoning one's self isn't easy. Also, paraquat generated in the U.S. will make you vomit immediately so you have a chance of surviving if you accidently ingest." She shakes the glass test kit. "There's no trace of dye or my test kit would be purple." She glances around the room. "The entire house will need to be disinfected by hazmat. The most important thing now, is notifying the hospital so they can begin treatment on your victim. My guess is she wore contaminated clothing so her clothes at the hospital also need to be isolated until we can recover them and have them checked. The items I tested came from her laundry basket inside the closet. Some hanging items are also contaminated or at least I believe they are. I'll know for sure after I test them."

My thoughts go to Melony's rambling to her mother about clothing. The pieces of the puzzle clicking into place. My radio and cell phone are in my vehicle where investigator Lott told me to leave them but my hand goes to the outside of my suit where my pocket would be anyway.

"If you're lucky, it will be at least an hour before you're decontaminated. Use my phone to call the hospital." Investigator Lott hands me his phone.

It's covered in plastic and thankfully works with my gloves. I call dispatch and have them patch me through to the hospital since I don't readily have the number. It takes a few minutes before Doctor Timmons comes on the line. I relay what I have using a too loud voice so I can talk through the spacesuit.

"The patient has gone into rapid decline and we've just put her on a ventilator this morning. Last night, she was placed on dialysis," he says after I finish speaking.

"Do you think she has a chance of recovering?" I ask carefully.

"We'll know in the next twenty-four hours. A few minutes ago, I didn't think so. I've been doing my own research and came across paraquat. There is no antidote and treating the symptoms is all I can do. The only real hope she has is that she didn't ingest the poison. If that were the case, she would already be dead."

The call ends and I give the news to the hazmat team.

"Do you have enough to arrest?" Sam asks.

I shake my head quickly running through what I think happened and what I can prove happened. "It's all circumstantial right now. I'll write up a search warrant for my suspect's home and also for the tomato plant where he works. If the plant has paraquat from outside the country, I assume it's illegal?"

"It is," Sam assures me.

I actually liked Mr. Dapple and hope the tomato plant isn't closed down.

CHAPTER EIGHT

It's two hours before I finish taking pictures and go through decontaminating procedures inside the back of the hazmat van and it's safe to leave. I head back to the police department to give Bell a break and then start writing more search warrants.

An hour into typing, my phone rings and our secretary informs me Stephanie Eaton is on line two. I take the call and she wastes no time coming to her point.

"I just spoke to Melony's mom. If you haven't locked Beau up, I'm going after him."

I rub the bridge of my nose. "If you go after him, I'll arrest you for inhibiting a felony investigation which if you didn't know, is a felony. I understand your distress but you will allow me to do my job without threats from you. Am I understood?"

She starts crying and finally replies in a softer tone. "Don't let him get away with this."

"I have no intention of doing that. This case is my number one priority. I need time so the charges aren't thrown out once I make an arrest. The best way you can help is to allow me to do my job and keep town gossip at a minimum." My tone is also softer. I don't have time for Stephanie and she needs to understand her threats only complicate matters.

She sniffs a few times. "I'm trusting you, Detective Jolett. I can't lose my best friend."

A small crack forms in my heart for Stephanie. I look at Bell and take a deep breath. "I know what it feels like to lose your best friend." I don't tell her mine was a K9 named Suii. I also don't tell her that his loss still hurts even though I have a new best friend.

"Thank you, Detective." She hangs up and I go back to my warrants.

By the time they're ready, I can't find a

judge to sign them and use the cell number John Eship gave me years ago if this happened.

"You bag em, I tag em," he answers.

"Judge Eship?" I ask skeptically.

"I take it this is official," he says with a laugh.

"This is Detective Jolett. I need warrants signed and there isn't an available judge at the courthouse. Is there any chance I could bring them to you?"

"I need dinner. Meet me at Mom's Diner in thirty."

He hangs up and I look at Bell. "You bag em, I tag em? We could have a serial killer judge on our hands."

Bell's tail thumps against the floor.

"You want a Mom's burger, don't you?" I ask.

Her tail thumps harder and we're both in agreement. My hips can stand a hamburger at this current time and Bell is okay with having gas throughout the night. I would say a win for both of us, but I'll be on the receiving end of her disgruntled stomach. I will most likely change my mind about the burgers at some point during the night, but right now my stomach is growling.

Mom's Diner is tucked away in the center of town behind the drugstore. During the hot Arizona summers, our town gets its share of tourists who want to beat the heat. Mom's is considered a local-only restaurant, though out of town travelers do find it on occasion. Mom's makes the greasiest hamburgers on the planet and also the best-tasting. We will pay but it sounds so much better than a TV dinner.

The restaurant isn't crowded when I arrive with Bell at my side. Our favorite back corner table is available and we grab it and wait for the judge. I order three waters and they arrive with Judge Eship. He looks questioningly at the water glasses.

"Bell gets thirsty after her burger."

He smiles, leans down, and gives Bell's scruff a solid scratch. She ignores him and keeps her eyes on me so I'll order something for her besides water.

"That dog has you trained," he says with a laugh.

"I told her she could have a burger and

she takes her food very seriously. If I were you, I would sign the warrants and not give her a side-eye." My expression is bland but the judge sees through it and laughs again.

The waitress arrives and the judge tells her two tickets. We both know he can't buy my dinner and I can't buy his. I give my order after he takes the nightly special. He then digs into the warrants. He reads through all three with an occasional grunt. I added a warrant for Melony's cell phone. The judge's pen comes out next and he signs them with a flourish.

"Have them filed at the courthouse first thing in the morning, preferably before they're served so making them official isn't delayed."

We both know they need to be filed before the end of the day tomorrow. We also know the problems that come up and cause delays. I nod my head right before our food arrives. Bell is the perfect lady after I tear her burger into small pieces. She would eat it in one gulp if I didn't. Food is now all that's on our minds. We really don't talk because again, if questioned about this dinner, we will both tell the truth. We don't discuss the case at all.

Bell and I leave with full stomachs and three signed search warrants. I make calls from my car to line up the officers for tomorrow. Sergeant Spence is my first call. He doesn't answer so I leave a detailed message on his cell phone. Next, I call Gabe. I fill him in to see if he can help.

"You're in luck. I'm available. Where do you want me?"

"We need to serve the warrants at the same time. I'm worried about Beau's house being contaminated so hazmat will meet you there. Once I hit the plant, Beau will know we're after him. If I find no evidence, I can't arrest. We need to stay in contact. I'll have an extra officer with me to sit on Beau for as long as possible. Someone tried to poison Bell last night and it's not a coincidence. Beau has access to different poisons and we need to be careful."

"We'll have him tomorrow and hopefully he'll take a ride in my back seat."

I groan good-naturedly. "He'll arrive in one piece with no bruises or I'll sic Bell on you."

"He tried to harm one of ours and I can't make any promises."

Gabe is old-school. I know he would never hurt an in-custody but I want it clear he's joking. "Bell says you can only take a bite out of his butt."

"If that's the deal with Bell, I'll take it but she is asking a lot."

"Meet me at six at the department tomorrow to go over the warrants. I'll have a team ready."

"Ten-four, Detective Jolett."

"Ten-one hundred, Detective Macky." Gabe is laughing when I hang up. I just told him I was on a bathroom break.

I call Leo next. He barely waits for me to finish before he tells me he's in. "You left me dealing with old men and I need some action. This current case is for the birds."

"You want the house or the plant? I need officers for both."

"I'm with you. I'll stand by and look intimidating while you find what you need."

The testosterone is running high tonight. "I catch more flies with honey than vinegar," I say sarcastically.

"Don't worry, Jolett. I'll have honied syrup dripping from my lips and still look intimidating."

I'm so thankful Bell is female and I won't need to put up with this all night. I'm fighting a grin of annoyance and my tone only makes Leo happier. He's also laughing when we hang up.

The first signs of Bell's dinner make an appearance in the small confines of the car and it's time to get her home. I search the backyard before allowing her outside. Rat Cat isn't around. Bell does her thing and then searches the yard with me watching. It will be awhile before I allow her outside alone.

My bedroom is sickeningly ripe by the time I fall asleep.

CHAPTER NINE

Dispatch wakes me at two a.m. and even before they patch Doctor Timmons through, my gut says its bad news.

"I tried everything I could, but it was too late. Nothing we did helped and she died twenty minutes ago," he says stiffly. This isn't his usual voice and I can tell he's taking Melony's death hard.

"Have you informed her mother yet?" I ask.

"No, I haven't made that call."

"Could you hold off until after eight this morning. I'm serving a warrant on the suspect."

"Eight is stretching it but if it will help you get this guy, I'll do it and notify the nurses in case she calls."

Our conversation ends and I try to fall back to sleep. I love working homicide. This case didn't start off that way and it makes it harder mentally. I think about Melony's mom and her friend, Stephanie. I feel like I failed them.

Bell whines from the bottom of the bed and I lean down to rub her belly and let her know I'm okay. "It's the job, Bell, but it sure is easier when you come in after the death. I just feel there is more I could have done."

She licks my hand and offers her K9 dose of comfort. It helps. I finally fall asleep until the alarm goes off.

This morning, there's no poison waiting in the backyard and Bell's able to growl at the cat while I get dressed. If someone tosses something over the wall with Bell out there, she'll alert me with more than a growl.

I drop off the warrants at the courthouse and have them officially stamped, thankful one of the clerks let me in early. I also hand over my return warrant information from yesterday. I was always told police do tons of paperwork. Detectives have more.

I have nine officers for the warrants along with myself, Sam, and Investigator Lott. Sam is coming with me and Lott is going with Gabe. Both men from hazmat will have a **chromatograph and spectrometer.** Hopefully taking Beau into short-term custody while the search warrant happens will turn into long-term custody.

Bell can't be with me at the plant and she gives me sad eyes when I leave her behind. It's bothering me that I still don't know the name of the poison thrown over my back fence. If I were thinking correctly, I would have had hazmat examine the meat. It's too late now.

My team arrives at the plant five minutes before eight. We drive three unmarked cars in case Beau arrives after us. The door to the small front building is unlocked so I enter and ask the secretary for Mr. Dapple. The men stay outside but she can see them behind me when I open the door. Her eyes show anger more than they show warmth so I know where she stands.

The attitude doesn't surprise me. The

plant employs prisoners and the workers, even the secretary, is protective. I'm sure this isn't the first time they've been hassled by cops. I'm actually thankful the plant lies within the county and not the city.

Mr. Dapple is just as cautious when he sees me and the warmth from the day before is absent. I don't give him time to ask what I'm there for. "I need to speak with you privately," I say with authority.

He does an about-face and I follow him to his office. "I'm unsure why you are hassling one of my employees, Detective Jolett," he says in an extremely annoyed tone.

"If you will give me five minutes, I'll explain everything. I need your help."

He hesitates a moment before speaking. "I make no promises."

I give the highlights of the case including finding paraquat at Melony's home. I add the information that this is now a homicide investigation and hand the tomato plant warrant over. This time Mr. Dapple does not need time to answer. "Beau orders items from time to time," he sighs and I can tell his brain is catching up with the fact Beau is involved. "We do not use paraquat here but he would have access to ordering it."

I inhale slowly. Mr. Dapple is going to help me. My eyes go to the clock on his wall. "What time does Beau start work?"

"He begins his day at eight but he's always early." He checks his watch. "Right now, he should be in his office." He starts typing on the keyboard in front of him. "I want to check invoices. We have one company located outside the U.S. that would be a possibility." He turns the monitor slightly so I can see what he sees. He scrolls through invoices until one catches his eye and he zooms in. He highlights a word and Googles it. The results are gibberish until he adds the word "paraquat" to the search. Bingo. He reads the information aloud and points to a picture of a product listed under a name we're unfamiliar with, thus the Google search. "This paraquat is illegal in the U.S.," he says. "Beau ordered it two months ago and this is not my signature on the purchase order."

"Can you print the order for me? If there is an original hard copy, I need to take it as evidence."

"I understand." He looks dejected and at the same time, he doesn't question helping me. I'll remember this. Mr. Dapple did hard time at Perryville and he has no interest in doing more. I respect what he's done with his life. I wasn't lying about learning something from him. He changed and it is possible. It's something I needed to witness.

"I have officers outside to help with the warrant. I need them to know it's safe and I would like one of them to accompany us to Beau's office along with a hazmat specialist."

He scratches his cheek. "Call them. I can't believe Beau ruined his life this way. He's a solid employee as I told you before." He shakes his head. "That poor woman. I'll do everything I can to help."

I call Leo while Mr. Dapple notifies the secretary to bring them back. Once my team is together, Mr. Dapple leads us through an indoor greenhouse. The men working turn and stare. This is not a friendly environment for cops and I keep my eyes peeled while thinking it would be nice to have Bell with us. We head outside to a larger outdoor garden section that has small buildings surrounding it. Dapple turns the handle on one of the doors but it's locked.

"Strange," he says and takes out a set of keys and opens the door.

The light is off and Mr. Dapple calls inside. "Beau. Are you in there?"

The office remains quiet and Mr. Dapple takes a step in. I place my hand on his arm. "The office needs to be checked by hazmat first."

Sam walks forward in his protective gear and enters with his chromatograph and spectrometer. I stand clear. First, he flips on a light switch, then looks over his shoulder. "This will take a few minutes."

I nod and he goes inside.

Leo watches everything going on without comment. He isn't happy about missing the chance to place handcuffs on beau but he'll survive.

Five minutes later, Sam sticks his head out the door. "There's paraquat in his desk.

It's packaged in the original container and I'm removing it. He was nice enough to leave the label on. I'll check the rest of the office before you enter. There's a small storage room in the back."

I turn to Mr. Dapple. "Can you find out if Beau came to work today?"

He nods and makes a call. The rest of my crew is keeping watch at our backs. They also felt the cool gaze of the workers.

I wait until Sam walks out with a black plastic-covered container about six inches in length. My mind jumps to Officer Conners handling the poison in my backyard. I'm an idiot. I quickly send Conners a text and tell him he needs to be seen by a doctor. The fact the cat is still alive gives me hope that paraquat was not used at my house.

My heart is thumping when I finally enter Beau's office and look around.

"I took photos," Sam tells me. "I'll send you copies."

"Thank you for your help," I say.

Mr. Dapple breaks in. "Beau hasn't arrived and he hasn't called in sick. He knows something is up."

I call Gabe. "We have paraquat in Beau's office and he didn't show up for work."

"He's not at the house either," he offers.

"I'm putting an ATL out and when I'm done here, I'll get an arrest warrant from the judge."

"We haven't found anything so far. Your hazmat investigator went in with his fancy machines but nothing turned up but a little marijuana."

"Call the drug task force and see if they want to do their own search warrant for drugs. At this point, a small amount of marijuana isn't priority for me."

"Gotcha, Detective,"

"Thank you, Detective."

"Keep me up to date and I'll let you know when we clear the house or if Beau shows up."

Our conversation ends and I look at Mr. Dapple. "I need to speak to his friends here at the plant. One of them might know where he is."

He shakes his head. "Honestly, I'm not

sure they'll help but you can try. I need to notify the owners as soon as possible. Will there be repercussions for the plant?"

"You've cooperated," I assure him. "I have nothing at this point that shows anyone other than Beau's involvement. I do need to question those employees though."

"I'll help where I can."

Even with Mr. Dapple on my side, I learn nothing new. Leo isn't happy that he had no one to tackle. He makes it known that I owe him for running a rosy warrant that required no tactical team. He's grumbling about old men when he drives away with the other officers who agreed to help.

CHAPTER TEN

The following morning, I ask Gabe to join me in Sergeant Spence's office.

Gabe appears tired but that's par for the course in detective work. He's well fed at home by his wife of forty years, though he's still in decent shape. Far too young to retire, I tell myself.

"I have a nationwide warrant out for Beau's arrest. I even did some fast talking at the county attorney's office for them to guarantee funds for extradition," I tell Gabe and the sergeant.

"Why did the county give you trouble over extradition?" Gabe inquires with a grimace. It's those types of hassles that drive us crazy and every government department has them.

"They felt Beau is dangerous but the person he's most dangerous to is deceased so the threat he poses isn't as imminent. Bottom line, they're worried about funds and say their budget is tight." Gabe rolls his eyes. "Conners called me this morning and we have a positive back from the poison thrown over my fence. It was rat poison and available pretty much everywhere."

Gabe gives a short chuckle. "It just so happens he had some at his house and I confiscated it, just in case."

I smile. "We'll have it tested to see if the batches match. I should also receive a rundown of Melony's texts and phone calls in the next day or so."

"Do you have any idea where he could be hiding?" Sergeant Spence asks.

I shrug. "That's the million-dollar question. His friends at the plant aren't talking and really, they may know nothing. My victim's mother has no clue and the victim's best friend will kill him if she finds him first. I was hoping for suggestions."

"He'll crawl out of his hole eventually." This from Gabe.

"My reports are written and the case is solid, I just need an arrest. Until then, I need another homicide to keep me from dealing with old men who haven't yet kicked the bucket." I bat my eyes at the sergeant. "I'll do almost anything," I plead.

He smiles. "You sound like Conners. He's begging for a detective position again."

Conners did a good job on my case and I actually feel bad for remaining silent. "He thinks JD is leaving. I asked and JD says differently," I tell the sergeant and Gabe.

"That explains why he's in my office five times a day kissing my butt. I'll give the chief a heads-up that Councilman Conners may be visiting him soon." The sergeant feels like the rest of us when it comes to Conners.

I'm going to regret this but I say it anyway. "He did a competent job on Bell's attempted poisoning and he acted professionally."

"Can I get that in writing?" asks Gabe with a laugh.

"Truth is truth even if I want to choke." I add an eye roll for good measure.

Sergeant Spence ignores Gabe's stabs at Conners. "You're back on homicide indefinitely, Jolett. I cleared it with the chief. You can help Gabe on his current case if nothing comes your way in the next week or so."

I smile at Gabe so my teeth show. "I'm all yours. Bell may take some convincing though."

"She's easy," he says with a grin. "A neck or belly scratch and she's eating out of my hands."

"I require a steak dinner but the outcome would be the same."

"Children," says Sergeant Spence.

Gabe and I grin. "Yes?" Gabe inquires.

"Get out of my office and do some actual detective work. Good job on the case, Jolett. Your suspect will show up."

Gabe invites Bell and me to lunch and we end up at Mom's for another greasy hamburger and another night of pending foul smells from Bell though she isn't complaining and neither am I. Gabe goes into a little more detail on his current case and we put our heads together and come up with a game plan. Due to cutbacks, we seldom have a chance to tag team a case though we do help each other when we can. It reminds me of working with Tony and my heart misses one small beat before I give all my attention to the senior homicide detective.

I arrive home at a little after six. With dinner taken care of, I put on my jogging clothes and place Bell's regular lead on. She could also use some exercise after the huge lunch-dinner combo we had. Our food has had a chance to settle so a run will be good for us.

A mile in, Bell is having a great time while I huff and puff. "You need to get me out more, Bell. I'm losing my endurance."

Bell doesn't show the least amount of concern when I loop around the next block, cutting our run in half, and head home. She also doesn't need to toss her hamburger like I do.

"Good job, Bell," I say between breaths. "Let's try that again tomorrow." She looks at me with her "that's ridiculous" dog face. "Or not," I add because I can tell she's calling my bluff. I hang her leash up and follow Bell to the back door when she whines. I don't need to look to know Rat Cat is waiting. Leaving Bell inside, I walk my small yard looking for strange objects. I have a pile of leaves in the corner that fall from the tree located outside my fence. I ruffle the leaves for good measure, then head back inside just as the doorbell rings. "Hold on, Bell, and I'll let you out to be antagonized by the cat. I need to see who's at the door first." I check the peephole. The old man I recognize, the woman with him, I do not.

It's a small town, I remind myself. People think they can come to any officer's home without an invite. It's happened before but once I fill them in on proper protocol, it doesn't happen again.

I open the door a crack. "Let me place Bell in the backyard and I'll be right back."

"Sure thing," the woman says in a chipper voice.

"May I help you?" I ask politely once Bell is occupied with Rat Cat. I don't feel polite but the woman reminds me of one of the older ladies who fostered me as a child. She was one of the few I liked.

The woman, with laugh lines around her mouth, turns and glares at Jeb Garland who is completely clean for a change if his damp hair and lack of obnoxious smells is an indication. She looks back at me and her eyes soften. She places her hand out. "I'm Mrs. Garland the unfortunate woman married to this old reprobate." She looks at least twenty years younger than her husband and she's also thin and could run laps around him if she needed to.

I shake her hand while practically choking on air I'm so surprised. She isn't done.

"I overheard a rumor in my quilting group that my husband was disrespectful to you. After speaking with him and getting to the truth, he's decided to apologize." Her eyes scrunch up and she turns the frightening eye-blast to her husband again.

Jeb is looking at his feet and misses the laser pinpoints. "Sorry," he says gruffly.

"You think that's good enough?" she gripes. "Think again. Look at her and show respect."

I could be in love. I want to be Mrs.

Garland when I grow up.

Jeb looks me in the eye. I see none of the bravado he showed with his friends. "I'm truly sorry, Ms. Jolett."

Mrs. Garland makes an angry sound much like a growl and her husband cringes. "That's Detective Jolett, you dip weed. You can't even get her title right but you will before we leave."

"Detective Jolett," he adds quickly.

Mrs. Garland gives me her full attention and her eyes are back to normal. "My quilting group thinks you're the bomb. If you would like to talk to the women in this community, please let me know. Our group would love to host you and your amazing dog too. Is there anything else you need from my husband before we get out of your hair?"

I seriously can't help myself and if I don't say something intelligent, laughter will win. "A name. I would like to know who shot Lucky's window."

Jeb scuffs the toe of one boot against the cement. "No, I don't know." He looks at his wife.

She raises her arm and smacks him on the side of his head. I've just witnessed a domestic assault and I'm unsure what to do.

"Give the woman a name or so help me, you won't go back to Lucky's and stay married to me."

"Maud," he all but begs.

"A name," she snaps out while killing him with her eyes again.

"It was Leroy but he was drunk and he knows it was stupid."

"Thank you," I say with a small amount of compassion. Even I would be afraid to go home with Mrs. Garland after this.

"We'll get out of your hair now, sweetie. If my husband or any of the old coots in this town give you trouble, you just let me know and I'll take care of it. The men think we women don't know what they're up to, but they're wrong."

"Uhh, thanks," I practically squeak.

She grabs her husband's arm and turns around, dragging him with her. With a last look over her shoulder, she calls out, "They're also cheating Larry out of coffee at

Lucky's and fill their coffee cups more than one refill."

"Ahh, Maud," Jeb whines much like Bell does at Rat Cat.

"Just try me again and I'll tell all your secrets." They continue bickering as they walk to their car. I shut the door, shaking my head. I'm unsure whether to laugh or call an officer to check on Jeb in case his wife decides to do real bodily harm.

I enter the kitchen and fill a glass with water. The doorbell chimes again and I sigh. I guess Mrs. Garland isn't finished torturing me or her husband. I open the door without checking the peephole. I'm only able to crack it a few inches when Bell jumps against the back door with a ferocious growl. A second later, the door is forcefully pushed toward me and I'm thrown back.

My instincts kick in immediately. Lifting my arm, I block just before the bat connects with my head. The blinding pain to my arm is instant and my brain goes numb for a moment. I have just enough mental function to shove my leg into the opening of the door to keep Beau from slamming it with us inside.

He grabs my hair before I scream and drags me back away from the door. I should have more fear for my own safety at this point because he pulls a knife. My only thought is for Bell if I don't survive. With Beau's sweaty red face and spittle coming from the side of his lips, he's completely out of control. If I can't get the upper hand, I'm dead and so is Bell. I feel it.

He slams my head into the floor and reaches back to close the door.

He isn't quick enough. Eighty pounds of ferocious killer launches herself at Beau, locking her teeth on his shoulder. I have no idea how Bell escaped the backyard but somehow, she did. Beau cries out and lifts the knife.

"No, you don't," I say and kick out, connecting with his hand. The knife flies toward me and he screams louder as Bell uses him for her teething ring. I manage to kick the knife farther into the kitchen away from where Beau is battling Bell. My forearm is broken but my legs and voice work fine. I see my neighbor Bill over the chaos, outside my door. "Call 9-1-1," I shout. The poor man is probably wishing they found somewhere else to live.

Beau falls to the ground screaming and I lift my legs bringing one down on his and use the other to scissor him. "Get 'em off, get 'em off," he screams even louder.

"It's a her, you idiot," I yell back. Stupid to point out but true. My legs, with Bell's help, have him trapped. She's simply holding on now and not actually trying to eat him but I can tell she's causing pain. I hear sirens in the distance and Bill comes back and places his booted foot on the side of Beau's head.

"Don't bite me, doggie; I'm one of the good guys," he tells Bell.

Scratch what I just thought. I like having Bill for a neighbor and I'm not too proud to take help. A minute later, we're invaded by police. "Bell. Release," I tell her. She lets go with a final growl and a few snaps of her powerful jaws.

Bill backs off and Conners grabs Beau, rolls him, and places a knee to his back while placing him in handcuffs. Beau moans but that's about it.

"He pulled a knife and it's on the kitchen floor," I say as I roll partially sideways, protecting my arm which has decided it wants to fall off because falling off would hurt less.

Bell licks my face and I uncradle my broken arm and pull her in close to me with the good one. Shock is beginning to set in and my fingers are shaking.

"Laci," Gabe says softly. I don't even know where he came from. "I've called an ambulance for you. Where are you hurt? Did he get you with the knife?"

"No. It's my arm. It's broken. My other parts are still in one piece."

"I'll let the ambulance crew decide that when they get here," he says with relief.

Conners takes Beau to his patrol car and returns. "I called a second ambulance but I'm waiting until you get a ride. He has teeth punctures but nothing that will kill him unless we get lucky. I'll stay with him at the hospital until they release him. I have everything I need for charging on the arrest warrant. Take care of yourself." He leaves to sit with Beau.

"Was that Conners, actually being pleasant and performing his job without whining?" Gabe asks.

"No, you must be dreaming," I say wearily.

"That's what I thought. I'll put it down to stress hallucinations."

The EMS crew and Gabe feel a ride in the back of the ambulance is called for and none of my complaining does me any good. Gabe threatens to bypass Sergeant Spence and call the chief if I don't behave. The only thing I win on is bringing Bell with me. I don't want her out of my sight. She saved my life.

Sergeant Spence arrives at the hospital about fifteen minutes after the EMS crew wheels me inside. He and Gabe refuse to leave even though I tell them I'm fine.

"You plan on staying the night?" Gabe asks.

"No," I reply stubbornly.

"How do you plan on getting home?" he asks sarcastically.

"Uber."

"Over my dead body." He looks at Bell. "Neither of us will let her get away with this and we have the sergeant on our side."

"Yes, you do," Sergeant Spence reiterates.

I close my eyes. "Just let me sleep and you can wake me in a week."

They both laugh even though I'm serious. Whatever they gave me in the ambulance for pain is doing its job. Unfortunately, the doctor enters and decides additional pain is required. He sets my arm which isn't covered by the aforementioned pain medicine. When I cry out, Bell growls from her place by my side.

"Are we going to have a problem?" the doctor asks.

"Only if you set my arm again," I tell him honestly. If he does, Bell can eat him.

"Just a brace until the swelling goes down. Does anything else hurt?" he asks while sizing the brace.

I don't mention Beau hitting my head into the floor. It was a solid whack but I have no ill effects from it. It's my arm that's screaming. "Maybe more pain meds?" I whine.

"Coming right up. Do you cry when given shots?" he asks, eyeing Bell closely, when the nurse returns with an injection.

"Bell. Bite the doctor," I command.

She wags her tail.

"I see she's a softy," he says with a grin in her direction after she doesn't do as commanded.

"A softy that saved my life. You'll be treating the guy she attacked shortly."

"Oh, he's here and he's crying like the baby he is. I'll be releasing him after dressing his wounds."

"Will he have permanent damage?" Not that I actually care but I do feel I should ask.

"Doubtful. Your dog tried to turn his shoulder into a tender steak, but I'm a wizard and can fix just about anything."

If I didn't hurt so badly, I might appreciate a doctor with a warped sense of humor. Right now, not so much. Thankfully, the shot does the trick. He puts me in a brace that will be replaced by a cast once the swelling goes down.

Two hours later, with a lot of complaining on my part, I'm released.

CHAPTER ELEVEN

Three days later, I'm attending Melony's funeral with my arm in the same brace the emergency room physician put on. One must go to the doctor to get a cast and I've decided it isn't necessary. I'll be extra careful and no one will be the wiser.

Funerals are not a part of the job that I enjoy. I wouldn't be here if Melony's mom hadn't asked me to come. I'm not good with small talk or condolences. I also feel insecure without Bell. This is the first time we've been apart since I went to the hospital.

I still haven't figured out how Bell made it to the front door. If she's able to jump the wall, the cat should be a memory. Unless I actually see her do it, I may never know.

"Please come by the house after the service," Marge offers when I shake her hand in the condolence line. She pulls me in for a hug and I accept it because what else can I do?

"Thank you, I'm so sorry about your daughter," I add softly once she releases me.

She sniffs and wipes her eyes before answering. "I never understood why she loved him. I would give anything to have my daughter back but she also holds blame. I think that's one of the hardest things for me. I would have done anything to help her."

"She didn't deserve this," I say sincerely.

The next person I greet is Stephanie. Her eyes are red and swollen. More so than Marge's. She doesn't hug me but she does offer a small apology when we shake hands. "I was upset when I spoke to you. I'm glad you got him and didn't test me, though."

"I'm glad too."

"Please come by Marge's house after the funeral," she reiterates.

Now I know I'm not getting out of it

so I agree. After the graveside service, I follow a line of cars to Marge's place. It's a small duplex on the west side of town about five minutes from the cemetery. Inside the home, every available surface is covered with food dishes. I'm told it was all handled by ladies from her church. I think it was one of them who informed me of this.

"Thank you for catching Melony's killer. You're the town's hero," a woman says to me after I've tried to find a corner to hide in without success.

I'm unsure how to reply because I'm so horrible at small talk and quite uncomfortable over being called a hero for doing my job. Stephanie, who most likely doesn't even like me, is my savior.

"She took a beating to do it too." She nods down at my arm and then smiles. "Her dog is my personal hero because she took a chunk out of Beau's shoulder. I'm just upset it wasn't his face."

"Yes," I say thankfully, ignoring the face comment. "Bell is the true hero."

"I was hoping I would see you here," says a female voice from over my shoulder.

I turn and it's Mrs. Garland. I haven't heard that Jeb's body was found so I feel comfortable saying hello.

"Mary," she says to the woman who just called me a hero. "This is the detective I told you about. She agreed to speak to our quilting group and anyone else we can find. She's bringing her dog and we'll get all the inside details on apprehending that horrible man."

I never told her anything like that but I'm caught. I am not a social butterfly who speaks to women's groups. I hate speaking to anyone besides Bell. Okay, Jack might be on the short list but even with him, conversation is painful. I don't get to voice my opinion though. Other ladies step into the conversation and the entire speaking engagement is planned around me.

When I look for a way out, Stephanie winks and walks off, leaving me to escape on my own. She really doesn't like me. It takes an hour to get out the door.

My cell rings before I can throw my car in drive and leave. I wouldn't risk being surrounded by crazy old ladies again but it's

Jack and I take his call.

"Hello," I say.

"Are you at home?" he asks cheerfully.

"I will be in fifteen minutes," I respond, slightly bewildered.

"Are you hungry?"

I ate nothing inside. "Starving," I answer again with more skepticism in my tone.

"You're in luck. It just so happens I have lunch for three and I'll be at your place in about twenty minutes."

"You're in town?" My heart rate increases.

"I am."

"The food had better be warm." I don't need to ask who the third person is because of course Jack will feed Bell too. He knows about the junk food I give her on occasion. I still owe her an extra special ice cream cone —no, two—for saving me and us solving the case. Maybe we can do that for dessert.

"I'll see you in a few," he says and hangs up.

Nervous jitters start in my belly. I have just enough time to shuck off my funeral pants and blouse and throw on jeans and a t-shirt. I open the door at Jack's knock. Yes, I check the peephole first. I still can't believe my stupidity over that one.

Jack, wearing much the same as me though he looks so much better, is holding red roses and a bag of food. My stomach flip-flops at the flowers.

He grins and thrusts them at me. "They're for your injury in the line of duty." He pulls a stick of some type from his back pocket and gives it to Bell who is wagging her entire backside. "It's an antler for her heroism and doubles as a way to keep her busy while we eat."

"Roses and an antler. How romantic," I say and then want to kick myself. Even I can feel my face flame.

He laughs even though sadness fills his eyes. "His Majesty went to his new home. I was feeling down and thought you might still be on leave for your injury and I was hoping to get lucky." Now it's his turn for a red face.

We make quite the pair and no, I don't read anything more into his statement than he meant on the surface. Jack has as much trouble with small talk as I do. When things like this are a problem, it's best to ignore the gaffes. Or so this antisocial woman feels.

"You inviting me inside?" he finally asks.

"Only if I can pretend this is a date." I have no idea where my bravado comes from.

Jack exaggerates wiping his forehead. "That's good to know. Asking someone out on a second date is so much easier."

We eat and we talk. It isn't hard for a change. For a first date, it's the best I've ever had. Jack has no intention of helping with an excuse to get me out of my talk to the quilting group.

"Think of it this way," he says with a straight face. "Talking to a ladies' group is community policing at its best."

"I'd rather face a firing squad and I thought you, more than anyone, would understand."

"I completely understand. I have a secret that works every time, though."

"You do? Please tell me." We're both relaxed and conversation is flowing like I always dreamed it could.

"It helps if you think of them as naked dogs. Just pretend they have furry bodies and you'll do fine."

I almost choke on my sip of soda. "I thought I needed to pretend they were naked, not with fur?" I question because I still can't believe he said that.

"You do things your way but I promise, mine is better." His smile is killing me softly.

"You hate me," I say and want to instantly slap myself.

Jack tilts his head and looks at me strangely. "No, I wouldn't say that's what I feel."

Thankfully, we changed the subject after that one. Jack understands me and he realizes this is entirely new territory for our relationship. Yes, I've dated a handful of times, but I've never had a steady relationship and never actually wanted one. Until now. Maybe.

After consuming all the food, we go out back so Jack can examine the wall. He nods his head at the corner where the block wall meets. "She staggered her jump, hit this wall, and then the other one to get out. It's something she's trained to do."

"Then why didn't she ever eat the cat?"

"I guess Bell likes cats more than we do. And even though I don't like cats, the last thing I want to do is eat one. Maybe Bell has a picky stomach."

"Not a chance. She eats hamburgers and ice cream cones."

"She shouldn't," he says with mock sternness.

I hold up my injured arm. "She saved me and if she wants hamburgers and ice cream, she's getting them. I'll put her on a diet if it ever gets out of hand."

Jack shakes his head and gives up the argument. We enjoy our afternoon and I finally question him about not having a dog to go home to.

"I had one. He died of old age a few years ago and I decided it was easier to bring home a dog in need of additional training without a personal pet at home. Someday, I might change my mind. A dose of Bell here and another dog there and I'm happy."

The man needs a dog.

Jack doesn't kiss me when he leaves. "About that second date?" he asks instead.

"Yes?"

"I have a week off next month. Maybe we could meet somewhere on the weekend and continue today's conversation?"

"I'd like that."

He grins and a thrill runs through me.

I watch him stroll to his truck and he waves when he drives away. I walk back inside with Bell. She looks as sad as I feel. I straighten up the house and then call our department's other homicide detective.

Gabe fills me in on the next court date for Beau. I missed the arraignment and Gabe went for me. Not that he had to do anything, it's just a sense of justice that makes us attend. "The pretrial is next Wednesday and it will probably not amount to much. The real meat of the case happens once we hit superior court."

Gabe tells me the phone company faxed over the phone records and there are hundreds of calls and text messages between Melony and Beau. "Expect a plea deal on this one," Gabe says.

Gabe also attempted to interview Beau after his arrest. Beau immediately lawyered up and we still don't know why he killed Melony. It's something we may never discover and Melony's mom is also left in the dark.

We did piece together some of Melony's crazy rambling before she was hospitalized. Beau brought her clothing from his house that belonged to her before their divorce. He rubbed paraquat inside. He knew exactly how to handle the poison and keep himself safe. From the text messages I received from the phone company, Beau told Melony he could only see her Tuesdays during the week. Marge told me he would do it just because that was her weekly date with her daughter and Beau hated their relationship and had always blamed Marge for Melony leaving him.

Most of what we know is speculation which is sad. Melony deserved better.

When it comes to Beau taking a plea, I'm good with it as long as he stays in prison for the rest of his life. Melony's death was premeditated and is a solid death penalty case. It's Marge's right to fight a plea, not mine.

I end my call with Gabe and dial Leo's cell.

"You still milking that injury?" he asks instead of answering his phone like a gentleman.

"You should be a comedian. I would be at work if the chief didn't tell me I was fired if I showed up at the office this week."

"Come on, we all know you're milking it."

"I'm hanging up now," I say petulantly.

He stops laughing. "Okay, what you got for me?" he asks.

I told him about Mr. and Mrs. Garland's visit after I returned from the hospital. "I was hoping you would update me on your senility case."

"I should make detective for this one," he says with more laughter.

"You don't want to make detective," I remind him.

"Leroy gave a full confession after I roughed him up behind the gas station. No worries, though. I made sure the video equipment was down for maintenance."

"Har, har."

"He paid off Larry and all's good. He didn't even give me a chance to rough him up. I think he was worried I would knock out his false teeth."

"You're all heart for not beating up an old man," I tease.

"He got lucky. Get it, Lucky Gas, lucky man."

"I'm so glad we aren't friends."

"Oh no, never. The one-woman detective squad doesn't need friends."

"Thank you for your help with the poison investigation and also for not throwing the book at Leroy."

"Now you're going mushy on me. I can handle your stoicism and unfriendly demeanor, not the mush."

We both laugh and it feels good. I do have friends and I also have the best K9 in the world at my back.

Before we end our conversation, Bell

starts sniffing and then whining at the back door. Jack didn't bring her people food; he brought her a cupcake from a dog treat shop in the city. My guess is her favorite hamburger would have agreed with her stomach more.

My call with Leo ends and I walk over to open the back door. I still haven't removed the wood block from her dog door. I'm not quite ready. Before I can open the door enough for her to go outside, I notice something moving in the pile of leaves in the corner. It's the darn cat. Except for when she was eating the bad meat, I haven't seen her in our yard.

I step outside and close the door before getting closer. Bell noses the door and bursts out just as I realize what I'm seeing. Rat Cat has a kitten. He or I guess, she, doesn't even hiss when Bell gets near. Bell goes down to her haunches and looks at me and whines.

Rat Cat moves a little and I realize she's having another baby. "Bell, we need boiling water and towels," I say because what the heck else do we do?

Bell inches forward and nudges the small wet kitten that's already come into the world.

"Okay, you stay here and I'll grab towels. I'm not sure what to do with the hot water so I'll pass."

I run into the house and grab every dishcloth I own from the kitchen drawer. The second baby has arrived when I return and Rat Cat is cleaning it. This one is black with a large white spot. The first was a replica of its mother. Over the next hour, two more make an appearance. Momma cat, who looks like a Tom, has no problem with Bell and me watching and caring for the kittens as she gives birth. One of the next two born is black with a white head and one is another orange tabby. I have no idea what their sex is because their little parts are swollen and they all look the same. Bell gives each a tummy lick when I turn them over like I saw someone do when I was young and offers no help.

When I'm sure Rat Cat is finished giving birth, I find a box and move her and the babies into it, then carry them inside my condo. I have no cat food and I have no idea how to care for a mother cat and kittens. There's only one thing to do.

I dial Jack's cell. "If this is to break our second date, pretend I didn't answer," he says as greeting.

"No, you need to get back here. I've had kittens."

DEAR READER,

Thank you for taking a ride-a-long with Laci and Bell. Like past cases in the Forever Series, this one hits close to home. I handled a paraquat poisoning as a detective. The case was quite eye opening and it was interesting to revisit some of the nuances I dealt with. On a side note: Paraquat was used in Agent Orange during the Vietnam War.

I enjoy telling you about things I change in stories and the Forever Enemy is no exception though I may enjoy telling you this more than I have in past books. I changed information about paraquat and poisonings in general. Why, you might ask? It's simple really. If you use this book to plan the perfect murder, it won't work. You will need to do your own research and leave a long internet trail for the detective who handles your case.

I'm sneaky that way.

When they gowned me to enter the home (on my real case), I neglected to ask hazmat for the name of the machines they used to determine the poison. Research gave me gas chromatograph and mass spectrometer but I could be totally wrong. So, if you're ever poisoned and they bring those machines into your home, please don't try and show off by using the above names. If I'm right (I did research it thoroughly) you've lost nothing. If I'm wrong, no need to embarrass yourself.

I mentioned changes in case law in this story. It happened often. One day we could search phones with a subpoena and the next day we could not. I spent a lot of time studying changes in caselaw and I'll be honest, it drove me crazy.

My victim was also in a safehouse and there is unclear caselaw as far as her right to privacy so, with her unconscious, I asked for a warrant to be safe. Often these small things pay off in the long run for trial.

I mention Bell and her bathroom habits quite a bit. This is something I learned when I rode with a K9. You must always keep their needs at the forefront. Things will get busy and your dog must be cared for regardless of the timing.

My next writing project is Suzie Goes to the Police Academy. I promise it's hilarious and heartwarming. It's based on the real-life me (fictionalized and cozy) and my adventures at age 45 when I decided to make my dreams come true and attend the police academy.

I'll also be thinking about the next K9 book and what to do about Rat Cat and her kittens. I do love adding my animals to the story and Rat Cat is no exception. When she was angry at me, she would pee in my tissue box when I wasn't looking. During allergy season, my red watering eyes would have me running for the box and promptly bellowing death threats to the cat. She loved to hate me.

I'm an email or message away if you would like to say hello or ask a question about one of the cases I've written about. I'm always eager to talk cop.

Peace my friends,
Suzie

Learn more about Suzie and her books:

http://suzieivy.com

http://twitter.com/suzieivy

http://facebook.com/suzieivypage

Newsletter: https://sendfox.com/lp/3qnpnl

Email: suzieivy@gmail.com

BOOKS BY THIS AUTHOR

The Forever Team

Meet Laci Jollett, a disgruntled detective without a partner.

When Laci's supervisor pairs her with K9 Suii, short for Suicide, she must navigate an unfamiliar set of rules and hopefully find a new human partner quickly.

Soon, Laci discovers there is more to Suii than she realized. As Laci uncovers the secrets in her K9's past service, her Forever Partner shows Laci the true meaning of loyalty.

This is a heartwarming story about friendship and loyalty. Parts of it may or may not be true.

The Forever Partner

Meet Detective Laci Jolett and her K9 Bell

Detective Laci Jolett understands pain and loss. In her detective career, two partners have died. Now Laci is faced with a new partner she's afraid to lose. When things heat up after a suspicious death at the local motel, Bell and Laci navigate difficult waters to solve the crime and form a Forever Partnership

The Forever Friend

The adventures of Detective Laci Jolett and her K9 Bell continue when Laci's neighbor has a heart attack and his little dog needs a temporary place to call home. When you're a detective who isn't exactly dog crazy, this could be a problem.

When two teens are sent to the hospital after taking dangerous pills, Laci must discover who is behind the school's drug problem before it turns into a death investigation. With Sugarplum and Bell's help, solving the case gets a little hairy and the K9s are put to the test.

A K9 is a detective's best friend and sometimes two friends are better than one.

ARE YOU LOOKING FOR MORE SUZIE IVY?

There's more fun and excitment waiting inside the Suzie Ivy Case Files.

Small Town Mystery One

Meet Suzie: Cozy with a Bit of Grit!

From amateur bookstore sleuth to police cadet, Suzie Ivy beat the odds and made it through the toughest eighteen weeks of her life. Join Suzie during her midlife wacky adventures on the streets of small-town USA.

With a shiny new badge pinned to her chest; hilarity and tears ensue. Add a Beefalo named Old Betty, crazy old men with rocks, and unlicensed drivers who think they own the road and you'll stumble along with Suzie while she takes law enforcement by storm.

Hold on tight, it's time for the Suzie Ivy Case Files.

Small Town Mystery Two

Suzie's wacky adventures continue...

The department's paramilitary on and off switch gives Suzie a dollop of trouble along with a certain old lady driving without a license.

As the summer heats up, so does a wave of crime that keeps law enforcement on their toes. From amateur bookstore sleuth to police officer, Suzie has a lot to learn and even more to prove as she finds her footing on the blue line.

Hold on tight, it's time for the Suzie Ivy Case Files.

Small Town Mystery Three

Suzie finally tosses the reigns of field training and heads out on the streets alone. Nightshift can be a desolate place when the other officer on duty doesn't give you the time of day. No worries, Suzie won't let anyone stop her from becoming the best officer she can be.

Changes in the police department hierarchy cause friction and possibly a new door for Suzie to step into.

This time, the Suzie Ivy case Files get real!

ABOUT THE AUTHOR

Suzie Ivy

 Suzie Ivy is a retired homicide detective who entered law enforcement at the great age of 45. She writes mystery, romance, and nonfiction under three pseudonyms with more than 50 titles in print. For posterity, Suzie would like you to know that people with three false names are usually criminals. In Suzie's spare time, she owns a martial arts studio where she teaches women to kick butt and stay safe. If she's not training or writing, you'll find Suzie in her garden surrounded by nature with her two dogs, Dizzy and Ava by her side. She's also married to a man of mystery. He's mysteriously put up with her for 40 years.

Made in the USA
Middletown, DE
06 February 2021